MANOR
OF
DEATH

THE POSSUMWOOD MYSTERIES BOOK 1

HOLLY DEY

MANOR

OF

DEATH

THE POSSUMWOOD MYSTERIES BOOK 1

HOLLY DEY

Manor of Death: The Possumwood Mysteries Book 1 © 2021 by Holly Dey. All rights reserved.

Black Mare Books

First Edition 2021

ISBN: 978-1-941502-05-1

Acknowledgements

I couldn't do this without the love and support of my wonderful family. I love you so much!

Chapter 1

DETECTIVE SERGEANT PC Donovan sat at the banquet table, wishing the congratulations-on-your-retirement speeches would end. Her back hurt and she had to pee. Lordy, she'd never heard such a long-winded Chief. It was an open secret that he had designs on the Mayor's office. But that was not her problem.

She sneaked her phone out of her uniform slacks and, keeping it discreetly under the table, turned off tomorrow's alarm. She'd get up when she got up. Perhaps go down to the art supply store and have a good look around. Painting, maybe some sculpting, photography—retirement sounded like a dream. PC would miss the people, but not the work. Twenty-five years in Homicide was plenty. She put the phone away and glanced at her FlitBit. Her sister had given it to her as a retirement present. Daisy had been so excited last week, making sure to tell PC that this gift—the one in the plain orange paper—was NOT for Christmas at least a dozen times. PC had laughed out loud when she opened the ersatz fitness tracker. Completely on-brand for Daisy.

It was her last day as a sergeant in Houston Homicide, and she'd make her step count by the time she got to the parking lot, if this retirement banquet ever ended.

She almost fell out of her chair when her phone vibrated in her pocket. A few people looked at her with glazed eyes as she got up and left the private dining room.

There had better be a good reason her sister was calling her. "Daisy?"

"You gotta meet me at the hospital. Mama's fell and busted her hip."

"Which hospital?" The rural county hospital where they lived had closed years ago, so she'd probably be coming into Houston.

"That one on the freeway."

"That doesn't narrow it down."

"It's the same one where she got that stent thing put in." At least PC knew where to go now.

"Have you called Rocky?"

"Don't know where he is."

That figures. She didn't want to call her brother a drifter, but if the shoe fit... He couldn't have gone too far–he was just at Mama's house last week for Christmas. And he wasn't exactly rolling in bus fare money.

"I'm on the way."

She texted a fellow retiree, Captain Hastings, to tell him she had a family emergency, and please give her regards to the Chief.

PC poured herself another cup of coffee. Her hands had finally stopped shaking, and the nausea had subsided, mostly. Daisy was in the ladies' room, fixing her makeup. There were windows in the waiting area, but they looked out onto the corridor. If they'd have been on the outside wall, she would have seen the parking lot and the freeway. Six one way, half a dozen the other.

I'm sure glad I bought that pee-pee station with the fake grass for Cordite. Poor dog would have exploded by now if I hadn't. She was glad her good boy would be waiting for her when she got home.

The surgeon came into the room. "Ms. Donovan?"

"Yes?"

She extended her hand. "I'm Dr. Liskova, and I did the hip replacement on your mother. The surgery went well, and I think Rose will be fine. She was… a bit dehydrated when she came in. Does she live alone?"

"She does. Why?"

"Sometimes elderly people forget to eat and drink, which makes them dehydrated, which makes them dizzy and more prone to falls. She's going to have to stay in a rehab center for physical therapy so she can learn to walk again. But you might think about having someone stay with her, or at least check in on her, every day, once she's back at home."

"Of course."

"The nurses will let you know when she's out of recovery and you can go see her."

"Thank you."

Five minutes later, Daisy returned. The eyeliner that had streaked down her face earlier was repaired, and the false eyelashes that had been hanging at crazy angles had been re-glued.

PC set her coffee down. "The doctor says Mama is in recovery. So far, so good."

"Oh, that's great news! When can she go home?" Daisy sat down.

"When she's done with rehab–"

"Rehab! Mama don't do no drugs! She don't drink, neither. Well, hardly ever."

"Not that kind of rehab." PC retrieved her coffee. "Physical therapy. Her body has to learn how to use the new hip. But when she's ready to go home, she's going to need somebody to look in on her every day."

Daisy pouted. "How'm I supposed to run the beauty shop, raise up two teenage boys, AND look after her? And all her critters? I *do* have a very active social life."

3

If you call hanging out at the Silver Dollar Saloon across from the truck stop a social life. PC crossed her arms. "Maybe Rocky could stay with her. Probably be good for both of them."

"I don't know 'bout that. He's got some… disreputable friends."

Of course he does. He's a transient. "Well, something's gotta be done."

"Happy New Year, Mama!" Daisy popped open a bottle of sparkling grape juice.

Rose Donovan's eyes narrowed. "It's 8:00."

PC handed her mother a glittery paper party hat and a noisemaker with glossy plastic streamers. "Visiting hours close at nine. I did bring a cake."

She'd picked up the dessert at the grocery store on the way. She pulled out the cake knife and quickly cut through some of the piped-on decorating. *I'm sure that s a champagne bottle.* PC had thought a quarter sheet cake would be way too much, but after a glance at her hulking teen nephews, Tyson and Zachary, she wondered if it would be enough.

"Mama, do you want a corner or middle piece?"

"Depends. What kind of frostin'? If it's whipped cream or cream cheese, then a corner. Otherwise, middle."

PC used a plastic fork to scrape a wad of "champagne bottle" off the knife and tasted it. *Buttercream. Middle it is.*

She set a square of cake on the tray table next to Rose's bed. Daisy added a plastic cup of bubbly grape juice.

"Dang it!" Rose dropped the TV remote in disgust. "I thought there'd at least be some fireworks or somethin'."

Daisy finished passing out drinks. "Well, here's to the new year! In with the new, out with the old!"

They all raised their glasses.

"I hope you're not talkin' about me." Rose sipped her drink.

Daisy's mouth popped open. "Of course not, Mama! Why would you think that?" When Rose didn't reply, she added, "Are they servin' you black-eyed peas with cornbread and cabbage tomorrow?"

Rose took another drink. "Don't know."

"I'm cookin' up a big batch, and I'll send some in with PC."

Thanks. The detective took a sip of juice.

She served up another four pieces of cake onto paper plates, taking one for herself.

Daisy waved her plastic fork like a magic wand. "Who's got New Year's resolutions? For myself, I'm gonna lose that pesky ten pounds and sell more color treatments at the beauty parlor. Mama, how 'bout you?"

Rose yawned. "I guess I'll learn to get around on my brand-new hip."

"All-star tackle this year," Zach said around a mouthful of cake.

Tyson gave his brother a light shove. "You better, 'cause I'm gonna set the record for passin' yards."

Daisy stared at her sister, then gave her a tight-lipped smile.

"Oh, I resolved not to make New Year's resolutions a long time ago." PC picked up a forkful of cake.

"Spoil sport." Daisy gave a disapproving shake of her head. "Zach! Tyson! Y'all come over here and we're gonna sing *Auld Lang Syne*. You, too, PC. Gather 'round Mama's bed."

A gravelly snort came from Rose's direction. The meds had kicked in, and she'd fallen fast asleep.

Hoping to get on the road and get home before the drunks were out in force, PC wished Daisy and the boys a happy New Year and dropped the remaining half of the cake at the nurses' station.

"Thanks for working tonight, and have a great New Year," she told the charge nurse.

PC stared at the ceiling. The same one she'd stared at for eighteen years, before she moved out of her mother's house. It was weird, sleeping in her childhood bedroom. Of course, she came to Possumwood to visit on birthdays and holidays. But it was a place she'd gotten out of as fast as she could, and she had no desire to come back. Too many bad memories.

Problem was, Rose had critters.

Four cats, two donkeys, a three-legged goat, and a flock of chickens to be exact. But who was counting? Somebody had to take care of all those animals while Rose was in the rehab center in Houston, and then for a while after she came home. That's why it would have been perfect for Rocky to come stay with their mother. She needed help, and he needed a place to stay.

PC rolled over and rearranged her pillow. Her brother was perhaps the one person who wanted to see Possumwood in his rearview mirror even more than she did. PC was scarred, but their father's murder had broken him.

For the twenty days that Rose Donovan was in rehab, PC researched elder care. Cordite supervised. He was twenty pounds, give or take, although it was probably on the give side since they'd been in Possumwood. She gave him too many treats, but it kept him from barking at the cats. Which was good for his health. Marmalade, the orange tabby, was almost as big as the terrier mix, and could easily shred him into tiny pieces. The other three cats would surely help. PC's mother pouted when the rehab center wouldn't let the dog come along with PC to visit her.

Home healthcare did come out this far into the boonies. But none of them offered livestock care as an option. Daisy might know of some 4H or FFA kids who'd be able to feed the animals to earn some extra cash.

Even after Rose got back on her feet, somebody would need to check on her every day, to make sure she hadn't fallen and was taking her medication. Daisy lived just on the other side of town, ten minutes away, tops, in traffic. But she was not exactly reliable. She was a good soul, and PC didn't think she would deliberately neglect Rose, but she was inclined to forget things, especially if they weren't directly about her.

That left Azalea Manor. Her mother was not going into a nursing home without a fight, though. PC had scheduled a tour of the facility for Monday morning. Then she was picking Rose up after lunch.

The detective pulled into Azalea Manor's caliche driveway and parked in the gravel visitor's parking lot. The rocks were too big to comfortably walk on, and she worried about turning an ankle as she made her way to the main entrance.

Paint peeled off the faux marble pillars that held up the sagging portico. The building looked abandoned. Had she come to the wrong place? Through the hazy glass door, she saw a nurse pushing a wheelchair down a hall lit by a sallow light. PC swallowed hard, then reached for the door handle and pulled.

Urine.

Institutional food.

Disinfectant.

Those were the most identifiable smells that assaulted her as the door screeched open. She turned to leave.

"Hello? Can I help you?" A woman in scrubs parked a patient in a walking frame against the corridor's handrail.

Caught! Dammit. "Yes. I have an appointment with the director. But I—"

The walking frame lady began to moan loudly.

"Okay, Miz Brazwell, we're gonna get you back to your room. You shouldn't go wandering off like that." The nurse handed PC a plastic bag. "Can you carry this for me, please?"

She put one hand on her patient's back and steered the walker with the other.

"Sure." At this point it would have been rude to say no. PC took a quick peek inside the sack as the nurse helped the elderly lady hobble down the hallway at glacial speed. Adult diapers. At least they weren't used.

Finally, the tiny parade stopped at an open door.

"You can just hang that on the door handle, hon. If you're looking for Miz Fennec, go to the nurses' station just ahead. They'll help you." The nurse guided the walking frame through the doorway.

"Thank you." PC slid the plastic loops over the protruding metal. Could she slip out without anyone noticing her at this point?

"Miss Donovan?" The voice came from a woman shuffling towards her down the hall.

Guess not. "Yes?"

The woman extended her hand. She was a large lady, but everything about her drooped and sagged as if her very skin was too tired to hold anything up. "Hi. I'm Durelle Fennec. I'll take you on the tour." She handed PC a manila folder. "The admissions paperwork is in there."

She doesn't waste any time. "Okay."

Director Fennec led PC the six feet or so to the nursing station. One nurse typed on a keyboard hooked to a computer with a green monochrome monitor. The building was shaped like an H, with the nursing station and some offices on one side of the crossbar. The cafeteria and common area were on the other. For security's sake, the entrance should have been there, too. Yet another reason to give this place a hard pass.

Fennec pointed behind the station. "That there's the gift shop."

Dusty knickknacks languished on glass shelves in the window.

"You can get a drink or a snack there, too. There's a vending machine if there ain't no cashier. We have a volunteer, comes in Monday, Wednesday, and Friday mornings to run the shop. If they do a craft, residents can sell it there."

PC nodded. She'd already made her decision and was working on her exit strategy.

Fennec pointed down the corridor where PC had entered. "That's our ambulatory wing." Her arm arced to point at the opposite end of the same leg of the H. "That's semi-ambulatory." She switched arms and pointed to the same end of the other leg. A glass door led to this wing. "Alzheimer's and dementia. We have to lock 'em in so they don't roam around and go outside. Your loved one don't have dementia, do they? Cause we're full of 'em. Cain't take no more." And finally, the last section. "Bed-ridden. Any questions?"

"No. I'm good. Thanks."

"Alright. Lemme know when you're going to bring your loved one, we'll get a room set up. The Medicare paperwork is in the folder. Make sure you get that approved first."

"Thanks for your time. I've got another appointment, so I've got to get going."

Fennec grunted and turned away.

It took a lot of self-control for PC not to sprint out of the building. A pall of sadness threatened to envelop her, even as it weighed down the residents. As soon as the door opened and fresh air hit her lungs, she sucked it in greedily.

Her phone rang before she got back to her car. It was Daisy.

"You gotta get home right now! Guinevere is missing."

Chapter 2

"What? Which one is Guinevere again?" PC's phone connected to the Bluetooth in her car and she dropped it onto the passenger seat.

"I don't know! I cain't keep track a all Mama's animals. But her neighbor, Mr. Youn, called me. He saw the gate open and shut it. but Guinevere was gone. And Mama had told him last time she got loose that Mr. Parker threatened to shoot her if she got in his roses again."

PC glanced at the dashboard clock as she pulled onto the highway. She had an hour and a half until she had to leave to pick her mother up from the rehab center.

"Which house is Parker's?"

"If you're standing on Mama's front porch facing Travis Street, you'll go south three blocks and hang a right on 14th. He's down that way a few houses–it's two stories, kinda tan with big ole rose beds."

"On my way."

PC stepped on the gas, then let off a little. She was a private citizen these days, and Possumwood was known for its enthusiastic traffic enforcement. She didn't believe Chief Wilson wouldn't cut her a millimeter of slack, given that they'd had a nasty break up in high school, and time had not smoothed over that seething pile of ugly. It was likely that eventually she'd run into him, but if she were really lucky, she'd avoid him altogether during her brief stay. Rose was done with rehab, so PC would probably be back home in a week, two, tops.

Don't get yourself shot, Gwen. Not on my watch. That's all I ask.

A smooth three-point turn later, PC rolled down Travis Avenue to 14th Street, scanning for an out-of-place farm animal in somebody's yard. Rose had two donkeys and a goat. She hoped Guinevere was the goat, because she could easily put her in the cargo area of the SUV.

Fugitive located.

The back half of a taupe-colored donkey protruded from a large shrub rose. PC sighed. How was she going to get a donkey home? The goat would have been so much easier. She pulled the car against the curb and checked for witnesses before getting out of the car. *Not a soul in sight.* And, more importantly, no one was standing in the front yard with a shotgun.

"Guinevere!" PC whispered.

A long, hairy ear flicked in her direction.

At least she's not a runner. PC was by no means an equine expert, but she did know better than to approach the animal from the rear.

"Alright, Gwenny. Here I am. Coming to take you home. Good girl." She walked around the rosebush to face down the donkey.

Guinevere raised her head, a pearl-pink blossom drooping from her rubbery lips.

"C'mon we've got to get out of here. Your mama–our mama?– is coming back very, very soon. You don't want to get shot, now, do you?"

The jenny blinked, her long eyelashes brushing her cheekbones and dislodging a few rose petals. And then she reached into the shrub for another bite, shaking the bush as she pulled off a mouthful of flowers.

"Guinevere! Stop that!"

PC didn't have any kind of donkey equipment–not a halter, not a lead rope, not even a dog leash in her car. She grabbed a fat handful of mane and tugged. The jenny was unmoved. PC leaned against Guinevere and pushed. The donkey swished her tail but didn't so much as twitch a hoof. Gwen was not going to budge without some type of guidance and encouragement. The detective ran her hand through her close-cropped salt-and-pepper hair.

I can't believe I'm going to do this. After a visual recon, she reached behind her back and unhooked her bra, then pulled each strap out from under her sleeves. It would have been a lot easier with a summer shirt. Using the undergarment as a loop around Guinevere's neck, she tugged and pushed. The donkey didn't budge.

"Gwen. Please work with me here. I'm trying to keep you alive long enough for my mother to get home. Please."

PC pulled Guinevere's head to one side. The donkey took a step.

Finally! She's moving. "Good girl. Come on. Let's go home."

Another witness check. So far, so good. They were almost to the curb. She'd have to come back for the car once she got the donkey back to her mother's. A beige Lincoln Towncar turned onto 14th street. PC looked down. With any luck, the driver wouldn't notice the bra's cups sticking up behind Guinevere's head like a second set of ears.

And that's where her luck ran out.

The car pulled into the driveway. A white-haired man got out and glared at her.

"What in tarnation?"

PC forced a smile. *If you have to walk through Hell, walk like you own the place.* "You must be Mr. Parker."

"Who are you, and what are you doing with that jackass?" He squinted and tilted his head. "Is that a black brassiere on that donkey's neck?"

"Yes, sir. That's exactly what it is. I'm Rose Donovan's daughter, and I've been taking care of her pets while she's in the hospital."

Parker chortled. "I shoulda known you'd be Rose's daughter. You Donovan women are crazy. You must be Primrose. I've heard a lot about you."

"You shouldn't believe everything you hear. But most people call me PC." She cleared her throat. "I'm really sorry about your rose bush. I can—"

He laughed again. "It's almost February."

PC blinked. *What does that mean?*

Parker raised his eyebrows. "Gotta prune 'em before Valentine's day. The harder I cut 'em back, the more they bloom."

So, all this was for nothing? He didn't care? "My sister was in a panic because she thought you were going to shoot Guinevere if you caught her in your roses again."

"Bah! Sure, I might dust her butt with some rock salt to send her home. But I'd never hurt Gwenny. You kidding me? Your mother would have my head on a plate if I ever did any harm to one of her pets."

Leave it to Daisy to get hysterical about nothing. When would I stop believing her?

Guinevere stretched out her neck and let out a long, ear-piercing *ee-awww-ee-awww-ee-awww.*

"I should probably get her back home. I've got to go pick up Mama."

"She's coming home today? Well, I'll be. Glad to hear that. You tell her the Parkers send their best, now won't you?"

"Yes, sir. I'll do that."

He gave another look at Gwen's lacy neck strap and chuckled his way into the house.

PC turned to the donkey with a withering look. "Alright, let's get this walk of shame over with."

Guinevere seemed happy enough to get back in her pen. Her one-eyed friend, Arthur, brayed to her before he came trotting up. Hazel, the three-legged goat, pogoed from the back of the paddock, *mmmaaaa-mmaaa-ing*. Even Clementine, the big orange Orpington hen, left the flock of smaller chickens to run over and see what was going on.

PC released Guinevere from her lingerie bondage and stepped inside to re-harness herself. The bra–that had been her last clean one this morning–was covered in donkey hair. She gave it a quick shake and got dressed.

Bong! Bong!

She didn't even have to glance at the grandfather clock to know she should have left ten minutes ago. And she still had to jog back to the car.

PC caught a strong whiff of *eau de Guinevere* as she got out of the SUV, but there was nothing she could do about it now. It wasn't too bad during the short walk from her RAV4 to the center's double doors. Maybe they wouldn't even notice.

She checked with the nurse's station, and the discharge paperwork was ready for her signature. She picked up the pen on top of the folder. The nurse's nose twitched as she raised her head and scanned the area.

PC focused on the pen. Click. Sign. Initial. Initial. *How many initials are there? This was worse than buying a car*. Click. Rose was now officially in her custody.

The nurse took the paperwork and tucked PC's yellow copy into the discharge folder. "Yes, ma'am. If you hurry, you'll catch the doctor."

PC strode down the corridor. Laughter bubbled out through her mother's partially open door.

"… Hazel's only got three legs, you know, but lordy, you shoulda seen her on that trampoline. That goat is something else."

Rose guffawed, and a male voice chuckled politely.

PC pushed the door all the way open. "Mama? How are you feeling? About ready to go?" She extended her hand to the man standing next to her mother's wheelchair. "Dr. Thompson."

"Miss Donovan. I was just telling your mother here that she needs to walk every day. If there is any swelling or fever, bring her in as soon as possible. Don't hesitate to take her to the ER if it's after hours. She'll need to come back in two weeks for her six-week visit, then for a three-month checkup. Most patients are fully recovered at three months, but a few do take longer."

Three months? But I hadn't planned to be in Possumwood that long. "Can I schedule that with the nurse on the way out?"

"No, you'll have to call the office tomorrow. Priscilla does all the scheduling, and she's out today. All the information is in the discharge packet."

Rose reached out and took the doctor's hand. "Oh, Dr. Thompson, I'm going to miss you. You're just cute as a bug. And my Primrose, she's single."

PC's cheeks flamed, and she wanted to crawl out the window. "Mama, you'll see him again in two weeks." *Maybe Daisy can bring you. On second thought, that might be an even worse idea. Daisy's the biggest flirt in Possumwood.* PC looked at Dr. Thompson's face without really making eye contact. "Sorry about that."

Then she tucked the discharge folder into the side of the chair, put her head down and wheeled her mother out the door. The collapsible cane that hung from one grip on the chair banged into her thigh with every step, but she ignored it. At least the plastic bag of Rose's laundry and toiletries that hung on the other handle wasn't going to leave a bruise. She just wanted to get out of the rehab center before her mother tried to fix her up with anyone else.

"Would you like me to push?" A nurse in pink scrubs asked. "I have to walk you to the door, anyway." She smiled.

"No thanks, I'm fine."

"Mrs. Donovan has kept us entertained with her stories about her animals."

"I'm sure she has." Tennies squeaked on the tile.

PC glanced down at the top of her mother's head as she moved along. Something was different. Was just the light?

"Mama? When did you get lavender streaks in your hair?"

Rose cackled. "You like 'em? They took me down to the beauty shop this morning, since I was being discharged."

"They're certainly colorful."

"I think they're beautiful," the nurse chimed in.

"Mmmm."

She'd seen hair like that before. Two years ago. Decedent had her hair bleached white, then added lavender streaks. She'd been stabbed thirty-seven times by her soon-to-be-ex-husband. Beautiful hair, the parts that weren't soaked in blood. PC remembered them all, each lifeless face that represented a death investigation. She shook herself to come back to the present.

The trio arrived at the front door.

The RN gestured to Rose. "I'll wait here with Mrs. Donovan, so you can go get the car."

"Be back in a minute."

PC pulled her SUV under the portico and got out to help Rose into the car. Once she was buckled in and her cane stowed, the detective took a deep breath and started the vehicle. The pink-clad nurse waved from behind the empty wheelchair as they drove away. Rose blew her a kiss.

"Have you been collecting those eggs for Justice to take to the farmer's market?"

"Yes, Mama."

"The green and blue ones get two dollars more a dozen than the regular ones. My girls are the only ones in town that lay after October. They shouldn't go to waste just because I'm laid up."

"Mmm. Chickens are all good. Your friend's been picking up the eggs every other afternoon."

Rose reached over and turned up the heat a notch. "And what about the cats? Sometimes Felix gets colicky when the weather turns."

"All fine." PC had been taking the don't-ask-don't-tell approach to Guinevere's morning adventure.

"What about Hazel? Has she needed a blanket? I didn't keep up with the weather much. There was a lot of medication at first."

I know. "Hazel's fine. Hasn't been cold."

Down to the donkeys. Which one would she pick first?

"Has Guinevere been taking good care of Arthur? She's his seeing-eye donkey, but sometimes they get into a spat. Just like an old married couple."

"Mostly." *Except for the part where she made a run for the roses.*

"Good." Rose looked out the window for a moment, then turned back toward her daughter. "Mostly?" Suspicion tinged her voice.

"Mr. and Mrs. Parker send you their best."

"Primrose Corvina! I told you have to push the slider *all the way* through and make sure the latch is *all the way* down. Guinevere can't get her lip over the latch if you do that, but she can open the slider in her sleep. She could have been stolen. Or hit by a car. Anything could have happened..."

"But it didn't. She ate a few roses, and I brought her home. Everybody's happy." *I'm not sixteen anymore, Mama.*

"Well, I'm grateful for that." She crossed her arms and turned her head away from PC to sulk out the passenger window.

Memorial City Mall flew by, then the Sam Houston Tollway. They were only a few freeway exits from the Houston city limits. PC was going to have to do something to appease her mother before they got home, or she would grump around the house the rest of the day.

"Mama, you want to stop at that new Brandee's? We could get some fudge and kettle corn." Appealing to her mother's sweet tooth rarely failed.

Rose sighed. "Well, I guess I wouldn't mind havin' a coke."

PC held an armful of fudge, popcorn, assorted baked goods and two bottles of soda water. They'd been here half an hour already, while Rose read each and every tee-shirt, perused the cookbooks, tried samples of hand lotions, and inspected Texas-shaped cast iron skillets.

"What about this? Might go good in the living room."

"Do you really need a mirror mosaic-encrusted cow skull clock?"

"Maybe not. But I *do* need some of that peach jalepeño jelly."

After nearly an hour, they were back on the road, Rose clutching her cow skull-free bag of goodies in her lap. They each had a soft drink in the center console and the open road beckoned. *Born to be mild.*

Rose crinkled her nose and sniffed. "What's that smell?"

"I don't know. What does it smell like?"

"Kinda horsey."

Thanks for that hair in my bra, Gwen. PC shrugged. "Mmm."

A few minutes later, she exited the freeway and headed north on FM 999. She'd always thought it sounded like a radio station–smooth jazz?–but instead of Frequency Modulation, the FM was a much less glamorous Farm to Market.

Rose took a big swig of her drink. "Getting closer."

"I'm sure all the critters'll be happy to see you."

"Not as happy as I'll be to see them."

Flooded rice fields shimmered on the left side of the road. A large flock of snow geese floated like heavy pack ice a hundred yards from the pavement. Smaller, darker islands of ducks staked out their own territory a little closer to the highway. Cattle sifted through brown winter grass on the right, probably hoping the clover would sprout soon. She almost ran off the road when she saw a pack of llamas grazing near the fence. A little further on, there was a wooden billboard near a gate. A grinning white goat provided the backdrop for the lettering: *Glenda's Fibers * All natural * Alpaca * Angora * Camel * Cashmere * Roving * Hand Dyed Yarn.* An auxiliary sign was tacked on to one corner of the billboard: *Now Open! Gift shop * Tea Room * Classes Available.* She wondered how many people came out to the middle of nowhere for afternoon tea.

Thirty-five minutes later, they pulled into Rose's driveway. Daisy's car was parked in the street. She and one of her strapping sons stood in the yard, holding a poster that probably said, "Welcome home, Rose!" But it appeared to have been hand-written in the car on the way there, and looked more like "Wehusre husre, Rusc!"

PC got out first and unfolded the floral print cane before she opened Rose's door. Daisy came over and got in the way so their mother couldn't get out of the car. Tyson remained in the yard, cell phone in one hand, and the now-folded poster tucked under his other arm.

"Daisy. Can you just stand over here?" PC gestured towards the rear bumper of her SUV. "And hold this." She shoved the cane into her sister's hand.

PC held onto the door while her mother pulled herself out of the seat. She was a little stiff and unsteady at first, but once she had her cane, she was a lot more stable.

"Oh, Mama! I'm so glad you're home!" Her younger daughter nearly bowled her over with a hug. As Rose struggled to regain her balance, Daisy chirped, "And you know who else is back in town? Heather Micah!"

PC shook her head. *What has Possumwood done to deserve that?*

Chapter 3

ROSE'S FOREHEAD WRINKLED. "Why on earth is she back here? Her mama died years ago, and her sister moved to Wichita Falls."

PC shrugged. "Looking for a cheap place to retire?"

Daisy's eyes widened and her mouth formed a little circle. "Wouldn't that be something? A real-life celebrity right here in Possumwood!"

A D-List celebrity. "The community theater group might—"

"Of course! People would drive out from Houston to see her." Daisy clasped her hands together.

Doubtful. "You don't even know how long she'll be here. She may just be passing through on her way to visit her sister."

Daisy planted her hands on her hips. "You're always such a Negative Nelly."

"Her biggest claim to fame was being the last one to die in that slasher movie. The one with the machete guy. Can't think of the name of it. And that was years ago." *I never watch horror films. Spent too much of my job cleaning up the aftermath of real-life monsters.*

"Would you two stop? Primrose, you've got the front door key, right?" Rose was making her way up the wheelchair ramp PC had had installed while her mother was in rehab. It was the only major modification she'd made to the house. She'd wanted to keep the work local and discovered a man she'd gone to school K-12 with, Bart Denton, owned a handyman service company. He and his son had done a superb job, and PC had enjoyed catching up with her former classmate while his son and a helper did most of the work.

The detective jogged up the three steps to the porch and unlocked the door.

Daisy looked at her son, standing transfixed by his phone in the grass, and huffed. "Tyson! Come over here and help your grandma. I raised you to be a gentleman!"

He hurried over, but Rose was already inside.

PC tossed her nephew the keys. "Tyson, would you please get that bag of laundry from the back seat?"

Seemingly grateful for a respite from his mother's disapproving glare, he scurried toward the car.

PC's dog capered and whined, wagging his entire body in excitement.

"Cordite! Be careful. You're going to knock Mama over, you silly dog." She tried to corral the furry menace, but he danced out of her arms.

Daisy scowled. PC was well aware that she didn't allow dogs inside *her* house and made sure everyone knew that. Her sister had not inherited the more-the-merrier gene regarding pets. Which was not necessarily a bad thing. Now that PC wasn't working crazy hours, she could be a budding cat lady. Or, more likely, a dog lady.

She had to dodge around furniture to keep up with Rose, who was headed straight through the house to the back yard to see the outdoor pets. A generously sized cat door led to a screened-in back porch, and that's where the felines spent most of their time.

"Felix! Marmalade! Sylvester! Chirp!"

The calico came trotting over, but the others ignored Rose, punishing her for being away, as cats so often do.

"Primrose, get me that box of cat treats from the pantry." She leaned over and scratched the undersized orange, black, and white cat. "Hello, Chirp! It's good to see you, too."

Who keeps cat treats in the pantry? PC hurried into the kitchen to look for them. She scanned each shelf but saw nothing cat-related. She slowed down and looked again. No joy. She turned and noticed a bright turquoise box poking out of the trash, begging for her attention.

She picked it up and examined it more closely. "Morsels!" in a bright yellow script floated above a picture of variously shaped rice crackers. PC had eaten them with a Greek salad last night. She'd needed just a little something crunchy to go with it, and the open box of crackers seemed perfect. They were okay–a little too fishy for her taste, though.

The light caught the much smaller font at the bottom of the box. "Cats can't get enough!"

Cats...? Oh, good. Cat treat/cucumber dinner. Yum. "I think they've all been eaten," she called out to her mother.

"You can't give 'em so many treats! It's not good for them."

"I'm sure they're fine."

"Well, maybe you can run to the store in a little bit."

"Sure."

PC followed her mother out to the yard. The chickens came running to see her, and she was able to lean over enough to pet the two largest ones. Hazel bleated and jumped around the pen. This woke the two donkeys, and they brayed as they trotted up to Rose. It made PC smile, even as she noticed the temperature dropping with the lengthening shadows and fretted about her mother not wearing a jacket.

Winters on the Texas Coastal Plain were typically cool, but not cold, with a few hot days sprinkled in for good measure–it was the south, after all. At seventy-five, Rose was in remarkably good health, but she was still more frail than she used to be. Convalescing for the past three weeks probably hadn't made her stronger, even if she was doing physical therapy.

"I'll just feed, then we can go inside, Mama."

"I can do it."

"Mama, you don't want to trip up Hazel with your cane, do you? With three legs, her balance isn't so good."

Rose opened her mouth, then closed it. She sighed and gave Guinevere a final kiss. "I'll put out some food for Blossom."

"Sounds like a plan."

Blossom the opossum lived underneath the screened-in porch, and Rose fed her with table scraps and cat food. PC had also noticed some robust raccoons loping in for a share of the bounty, so she put out extra cat chow. Blossom was usually gone by the time those pushy trash pandas arrived. Cordite either tolerated or didn't notice the marsupial, but the raccoons drove him mad. It didn't help that they taunted him through the window.

PC doled out feed and locked the chickens in the coop. The cat food kept the other visitors full enough that Blossom and the 'coons—chicken eaters all—didn't put much effort into breaking and entering the henhouse for an epic crime spree. When PC got back inside, she found Daisy on the loveseat, chattering away about Heather Micah, Tyson in the recliner with his phone, and Rose on the sofa where Cordite lay next to her with his head in her lap.

"I need to take my dog for his evening jaunt around the neighborhood. You want to go, Mama, or did you get your walking in at Brandee's?"

"I'll go with you."

Daisy looked stricken. "I guess if ya'll don't need us, we'll be on our way," she sniffed. "Dinner ain't gonna cook itself."

For the first third of the walk, Rose appeared to be surveying the neighborhood and gathering her thoughts.

"Primrose? I wanna go to Reverend Deen's Thursday night service."

"Oh?"

"It's not at the church. It's at the nursin' home. All about healin' the sick. Sometimes he even does a layin' on a hands."

Cordite paused to make a deposit.

PC pulled a bag from the dispenser on the leash handle and picked up the pile.

"If you really want to go, I'll take you. What time?" She shuddered at the idea she'd even considered putting her mother in that place. It was hard to imagine a social event there.

"After supper time. Seven o'clock."

PC knotted the end of the bag and dropped it into an open trash bin that had been set out for early morning collection.

"Are you in a lot of pain, Mama?" *Why else would she feel she needed divine intervention?*

"No, not more than expected–a lot less than when I fell. It couldn't hurt to get a little extra blessing, though."

"If you think it'll help."

"You remember Joshua Deen from high school? He was the quarterback the first time ever the Possumwood Panthers made it all the way to state."

"Yeah. We didn't exactly hang out. He was pretty broken up when Heather Micah got on a Greyhound bus for Hollywood the day after graduation." *Might be interesting if they run into each other.*

"Oh, I remember that. His mama was in my knitting circle. He joined the military the next week. Forget which branch. She passed a couple of years ago, you know."

PC spared him a quick thought, grateful her mother was still on the right side of the dirt.

On Wednesday afternoon, Rose's phone rang. Cordite, curled up next to her, raised his head, gave a single, half-hearted woof, then resumed his nap.

"Hi, Lin… You did?… Oh, my goodness!… Congratulations! Of course, we'll go… Bye."

PC put down her book. *What am I getting signed up for now?*

"Lin Youn, my next-door neighbor, have you met the Youns? Anyway, she got one of her paintings in the show at the art gallery downtown! There's a wine and cheese thing tonight–I told her we'd go."

"I wasn't aware that there was an art gallery downtown."

"Primrose, you haven't lived here in a long time. There's all kinds of cultural institutions here now."

PC raised an eyebrow.

"There's fine dining at *Truffles!*, a fancy antique shop, that craft beer place. You remember that broken down old Victorian across from the town square? That's been all fixed up, and it's now a bed & breakfast *and* a wedding venue. Happily Ever Afters, they call it. It's been featured in the Lifestyle section of the Houston paper." Rose nodded for emphasis.

"Still haunted?"

Rose massaged Cordite's ear, shaking her head. "They were sayin' that when I was a kid. Doesn't make it true."

"I'll get in the shower."

PC hoped that slacks and a long-sleeved polo shirt were appropriate for a wine and cheese event at a small-town art gallery, because that's all she had.

"Hurry up, Primrose! It starts in ten minutes!" Rose called.

"Be there in a sec."

She finger-combed her damp hair as she bustled out of her bedroom.

Rose stood by the front door. "I don't want to be late."

It'll take longer to get you in the car than it will to get there. "Let's go, then."

Surrounding the courthouse, the square on this side consisted mostly of the sort of shops found in small Texas towns, with the store fronts raised a few feet off the street level, requiring steps at either end of the block. The buildings huddled together, some separated by narrow alleys, most not, but each was its own separate structure, not a single subdivided construction, like modern strip centers. Wooden awnings supported the businesses' signs on top and shaded pedestrians below. The courthouse, built in 1872, sported a well-polished, brightly lit historical marker. A mirror image of the courthouse square lay on the other side of a two-block sized city park and housed city buildings.

Chunky, wild-west letters announced that *The Best Little Art Gallery in Texas* was through the well-lighted doors of the shop below the sign. Bare lightbulbs dangled from light strings hung under the awning in front of the gallery.

PC rolled her eyes. *Hokey.*

She held the door for her mother, who was almost instantly embraced by an Asian woman. A dapper older man stood next to her.

"Lin, I'm so proud of you! Let's see it." Rose took Lin's arm, and the gentleman steadied her elbow, leaving PC to trail behind them. She frowned. *Mama seems to be awfully familiar with that guy.*

"This one." Lin gestured toward a gorgeous watercolor of a peach-colored chrysanthemum.

"That's beautiful," PC offered.

"Georgia O'Keefe, eat your heart out." Rose grinned. "Lin, have you met my daughter, Primrose? She's been taking care of the critters while I've been away."

Lin extended her hand. "Nice to meet you. I've seen you feeding the animals."

PC took her hand. "Nice to meet you, too."

Rose turned to the gentleman and held his eyes for just a little too long. "This is Terry."

Terry bowed slightly. PC reached out to shake hands. "It's nice to meet you." *Can't say I've heard a lot about you.*

He captured her hand in both of his. "The pleasure is mine."

A tuxedoed waiter offered them glasses of wine from a silver tray. "There is a cheese board near the back, if you care to partake."

As they wound their way through the gallery, Rose introduced PC to every single person in the room and had a little chat with each of them. Some PC remembered from childhood, but many had moved in after she'd left.

Her mother's visiting gave her time to admire the pieces. She'd done some painting off and on over the years, but her retirement should give her plenty of time to work on her technique. Who knows? Her work could be at an art show someday, too.

"Drew! Drew!" Rose called.

A trim middle-aged man in black slacks and a burgundy button-down shirt with the top button open came over. PC was amused by his waistcoat–a fabric print of van Gogh's *Sunflowers*.

"Rose! I heard you were back home. How are you feeling?"

"Oh, I'm doin' all right. You're putting on such a nice show! Have you met my daughter?"

He took PC's hand. "I've not had the pleasure."

Oh, please.

"Drew Berlusconi, Primrose Donovan. Oh, look–there's Justice. I need to go see her." Rose hobbled away toward her friend.

"My mother is the only one who calls me Primrose. Everybody else calls me PC."

"Primrose is a lovely name."

PC felt heat rising in her cheeks. "Perhaps, but who's going to respect Sergeant Primrose, Homicide Detective?"

"You're a detective?"

"For twenty-five years. I just retired."

"Sounds so much more exciting than selling insurance. Something everybody needs, but nobody wants. I escaped into the art world after too many years of that."

"I've dabbled in painting, but I'm glad I don't have to try to make a living with it."

"You must show me your work."

PC took a too-big sip of wine. "Well, there's—"

The low murmur of the art patrons went silent. PC turned toward the sound of high heels clicking across the wood floor.

And there she was, in a form-fitting black-sequined cocktail dress. Heather Micah.

Chapter 4

HEATHER WAVERED ON her five-inch stilettos. Red wine sloshed out of her glass as one ankle nearly rolled out from under her.

"So thish is what pashes for culture now?"

Drew approached her. "Madam, would you care to sit down? Is there someone I can call to take you home?"

Heather's eyelids drooped, and she swung her glass up for another drink, but almost missed her mouth. "What, you think your little rinky-dink art gallery," she clawed two fingers of her free hand to make air quotes, "ish too good for me? Don't act like you don't know who I am."

Gallery patrons tittered to each other.

"I'm sorry. But you seem to be a little tipsy. Your safety is my only concern."

She tried to glare at him, but her eyelids kept closing. "I'm fa-moush. An influencher."

"How special for you."

She laughed and pointed to one of the paintings that wasn't included in the show. "That picture with the horshes. Ish that a Beltracchi?"

Drew's nostrils flared and his jaw clenched. Heather looked him straight in the eye and giggled.

Her glass tilted at a dangerous angle and Drew snagged it out of her limp fingers before it could spill.

She snatched it back, sloshing some wine onto the hardwood floor. "Don't. Take. My. Shtuff."

With a burst of unexpected coordination, she threw the glass at him. It grazed his sleeve before smashing on the floorboards, scattering glass shards around the deep red pool of Shiraz.

There was a collective gasp from the crowd.

Drew stiffened, and his eyes glittered. He took out his phone and punched in three numbers. "Yes, ma'am. There is an aggressive and belligerent drunk here at the art gallery. She's a danger to herself and others. Please send an officer to remove her before she hurts someone… Of course."

Heather shrieked with rage and lurched at Drew.

PC stepped in, grasping Heather's wrist with one hand and her elbow with the other, spinning the actress around as PC twisted Heather's arm behind her into an arm lock.

"Owww! You're hurting me! Let go!"

"Let's just walk to the front door, okay?" PC said through gritted teeth. She hadn't had to grapple with a suspect in a long time, but she was glad she'd kept up her skills.

Drew walked with her. "You. Are. Amazing!"

"I know," Heather purred.

"Not you." Drew shook his head.

PC quashed a chuckle. Heather had always thought she was the queen bee in high school. If she recognized PC, she didn't let on.

Heather squeezed out some crocodile tears. "Help! Help! I'm being kidnapped!"

People shook their heads and returned to their wine and cheese, no doubt tsk-tsking about how the mighty had fallen, embarrassed by the scene Heather was making, but relishing the juicy gossip.

Red and blue strobe bounced off all the parked cars. It wasn't surprising the police had arrived so fast–the station was only two blocks away.

But PC was surprised by who got out from behind the wheel.

It was the Chief of Police himself, Elwood Wilson. Her long-ago ex-boyfriend.

He eyed her coldly. "I heard you were in town."

PC nodded. "I have your drunk and disorderly." She pushed Heather a few steps in his direction.

"What was she doing?"

"I asked her to leave, and she attacked me!" Drew crossed his arms.

PC nodded to the crowd behind her in the gallery. "Whole room full of witnesses."

"She's hurting me!" Heather whined.

Chief Wilson's eyes narrowed. "Let her go. I'll take it from here."

PC released her grip. Heather pitched forward and nearly fell, only to be caught by the chief. She was close enough he would have broken her fall, even if he hadn't reached for her.

I'm sure that wasn't planned at all.

"She's all yours, Woody."

He regarded PC over Heather's shoulder for a long moment. "I hope your mama gets well soon. Wouldn't want you to have to stay here in town any longer than necessary." Woody then turned his attention to Heather. "I'm gonna take you back to your hotel so you can sleep it off, okay?"

He helped her down from the elevated sidewalk and into the front seat of his Tahoe.

Woody looked to PC. He paused for a moment, eyes widening, but he said nothing before he climbed into the vehicle.

"It was nice to see you, too, Woody."

He slammed the door and drove away.

She gave Drew a quick, apologetic smile. "Long time ago, lot of bad blood under the bridge. Best forgotten."

He nodded, holding the door open for her. One of the waitstaff was cleaning up the broken glass.

Drew gestured toward the door behind them. "He didn't even ask if I wanted to press charges."

PC shrugged. "She'd make bail as soon as she was processed, then she'd harass you and make your life a misery until her court date, where she'd likely get a small fine, if that. He probably saved you a lot of trouble. I'm just hoping she's too drunk to remember I was involved."

"Drunk. I wonder…"

Heather was gone, but so was the artsy vibe. People were more interested in Heather's melodrama.

PC excused herself to check on her mother. As she wove between clusters of wine sippers, fragments of conversations stuck in her ears.

"That Heather, she's something else…"

"… no one's called him 'Woody' since high school!"

"… Hollywood's ruined that girl. I told her mama…"

"… a little excitement is good for…"

Rose sat on an antique settee, upholstered in green velvet. Lin and the egg lady, Justice, stood around her.

"Mama, you doing okay?"

"Yes, yes. I'm fine." She giggled.

"You're not drinking wine with your pain medication, are you?"

Rose snorted. "I haven't had any pills in over a week!"

PC held up her hands. "Just checking. Making sure you're not too tired."

"Ha! I'm fine. Nothing better than catchin' up with friends."

"Okay."

The art show was half-way through, and PC hadn't looked at any of the paintings except for Lin's. She strolled through the gallery, admiring the work. All the pieces were flowers or nature watercolors. Very calm, very soothing. Heather Micah was all but forgotten by the time she reached the last painting. The crowd had thinned to almost non-existent.

"See anything you like?" Drew smiled at her.

"They're all beautiful."

"I think so. But now that woman is gone, perhaps I can get the focus back where it belongs and make these local artists some money."

"I was wondering how a small-town art gallery stays in business."

"I do get a lot of foot traffic from day-trippers out antiquing. But mostly internet sales." He sighed. "Let's talk about something more pleasant than naked commerce. You said you paint. I'd like to hear more about it."

"I said I dabbled in painting. There's a difference. I've been looking into signing up for classes, though."

"We host workshops on Saturday afternoons, if you're interested."

"I might take you up on that. Depends on how Mama's doing."

"Of course."

PC's car rumbled down the gravel washboard driveway of Azalea Manor. Cars overflowed the lot. Many were parked haphazardly on the over-long grass.

"Reverend Deen's Thursday night services are very popular." Rose gave a self-satisfied nod.

"Do you go every week?"

"No. Just every now and again, when my rheumatism acts up."

PC scanned for a parking spot but saw nothing even remotely close. She didn't fancy Rose's chances on the chunky gravel. "Alright, Mama. I'm going to let you out by the door, and I'll go park."

She pulled up as close as she could get to the entrance and helped Rose disembark to go inside. Two, or possibly three, spaces were available around back, near the dumpsters. The service started at 7:00 and they'd arrived fifteen minutes early, but it was dark now. A single light in the visitors' lot flickered a rusty yellow, only partly reaching PC's car.

She tried the closest door, but it was locked. Gravel crunched behind her. She whirled around.

A box fell out of one of the trash bins, and a flash of white streaked around the corner.

"Hello? Who's there?" PC made her voice as gruff as possible.

She waited in silence for a few heartbeats, but there was no further movement.

Must have been a 'possum. Or a cat? Raccoons would have scolded her for interrupting their dinner.

Her phone lit her way to the main entrance. She wasn't eager for the show, and less eager for the collection plate that would surely pass around afterwards. Joshua Deen had been a star quarterback in a small pool of small schools, but that hadn't stopped him from capitalizing on that glory run to the state championships for years after it had happened. Or so Rose had told her. Once

36

PC had put Possumwood behind her after graduation, she'd never looked back. Until now.

The place smelled more like Pine Sol than pee tonight, so that was an improvement. Rose was seated next to a lady in a wheelchair, but there was a single open chair on her other side. PC took her seat and cynically wondered if there would be popcorn to go with the show.

"Mama, are there always cameras?"

"Of course, honey! They show it on their website, for people who can't make it out to the nursin' home."

A woman in cat-eye glasses on a beaded cord squeezed the first notes of "Old Time Religion" out of a dilapidated piano. Reverend Joshua Deen, dressed in an expensive Italian suit, swept into the center of the room like a rock star. He raised his arms, as if to conduct the nursing home choir.

A scream ricocheted down the hall, bouncing off tile and wooden doors.

The music stopped.

PC leaped to her feet. From the first room in the far semi-ambulatory wing, a woman in a walker appeared in the hall. *Why does that woman look familiar?*

"Help!" she shouted, her voice cracking. "She's dead!"

PC followed the nurses, who rushed to her side. The woman pointed to an open door. PC stepped into the room, fully expecting to see an elderly denizen who had shuffled off her mortal coil during an afternoon nap.

Surprise forced a grunt from her slack jaw.

Heather Micah lay in one of the four beds, eyes open and neck bent at an impossible angle.

Chapter 5

HEATHER WAS MOST definitely dead. Of that, there was no doubt. The on-call doctor listened to her heart with his stethoscope but shook his head. The doctor had no trouble straightening her neck, so rigor mortis hadn't set in yet. She hadn't been there long.

But why was she here, of all places?

"Stay back." PC shooed curious onlookers out the door. "Don't contaminate the crime scene. And nobody leaves. Everybody stays here."

She pulled out her phone and dialed.

"9-1-1. What is your emergency?"

"I'd like to report a suspicious death."

"Yes, ma'am. What's your location?"

"Azalea Manor."

PC couldn't manage crowd control and talk to the 911 operator, so she hung up. Possumwood's finest would be along soon enough.

While she waited in the doorway, she carefully scanned the room. Four beds, one in each corner. Individual beds were outfitted with privacy curtains, but all of them were open. The bed closest to her did not appear to be occupied–there were no personal effects to be seen, and no sheets on the mattress. The bed on the same side, against the far wall, had a basket of yarn sitting at its foot. Half of a baby sweater was draped on one side, and a large bamboo knitting needle stuck out of a ball of yarn.

The bed across from that contained the remains of the late Ms. Micah. Aside from the obvious broken neck, there was no visible trauma. At least not on her face and throat. She was still wearing an expensive watch on the visible wrist. *Probably not robbery.* From the looks of it, the killer had covered Heather, and then the lady in the walking frame had uncovered her. Several large print editions of Reader's Digest lay on the nightstand, and one had fallen on the floor.

A single drop of blood, round and still wet, glistened luridly on the white tile. A narrow red streak lay not far away. Not a smear. Perhaps a contact transfer?

A stuffed animal afficionado clearly occupied the next bed. Teddy bears crowded the top of the nightstand. A stuffed giraffe stuck out of an open drawer. Plush animals of many species covered the dresser, but a small black cat with white paws lay on its back on the floor.

Two Possumwood PD officers, one young, and the other even younger, strode down the hall toward PC.

"Decedent's in here." She noticed a lack of evidence collection supplies. "Do you, uh, have a crime scene kit? Is there a photographer coming?"

The older of the two said, "Now, ma'am. People die at nursing homes all the time. It's a sad fact of life. Is this a relative of yours?"

"No, It's Heather Micah. But most natural deaths don't break their own necks and tuck themselves into someone else's bed."

The older officer tried to rush past her into the room.

"What are you doing? You're going to contaminate the scene. You don't even have gloves."

"Ma'am, this is real-world police work, not CSI."

PC rolled her eyes. "Sweetie, I've been working crime scenes longer than you've been alive. I'm just trying to help you not screw up."

The younger officer glanced at PC. "Bourgeois, go get the tape and those bags out of the car."

"Why don't you get it?"

"You got the keys, bruh."

Bourgeois scowled and stumped off.

The younger officer smirked as he watched his partner go. "I'm Tran. Hiro Tran. I'm guessing you're Sergeant Donovan."

PC cocked her head. "Yes, I am. That's a pretty lucky guess." *Especially for someone who looks like they should be in high school.*

"Chief's mentioned you... once or twice."

"Has he? Well, don't believe everything you hear."

Tran pulled a pair of nitrile gloves out of his back pocket. "I looked you up. 92% clearance rate. Impressive."

"Thanks. But I'm retired now. Twenty-five years in homicide is a long time. I'm happy to let you all handle things."

Tran slipped on the second glove. "Would you object to, possibly, consulting?"

PC almost laughed. "Not necessarily, but I expect Chief Wilson would strongly object."

"He might. But Heather Micah... local celebrity. There's going to be so much pressure to get this one right." Tran shook his head, sucking his teeth. "We don't get a lot of homicides here."

There's at least one other I can think of. "I'm sure Chief Wilson has the phone number to the Texas Rangers. They have some talented investigators. I've worked with them many times over the years."

"Oh, I believe that. Yes, ma'am. But they can't investigate if they aren't called. That's all I'm saying."

Bourgeois had come back into the building, carrying what looked like a large manila envelope and a roll of yellow crime scene tape.

"I look forward to reading about you making an arrest. I admit it–I'm curious. But I don't envy you–the list of people who didn't hate Heather is probably a lot shorter than the ones who did. But, not my circus, not my monkeys. I'm sure you'll do just fine. I'm going to go wait with the other witnesses." PC couldn't help herself. She leaned closer to Tran and said, "Don't forget to bag that stuffed cat to check for a fiber match on any suspect's clothing and look for latent prints on the magazines by the bed and on the floor."

She smiled and left to find her mother.

"Primrose! Is it true? Is Heather Micah really dead?"

"Yes, Mama. It's true."

"Well, you're gonna investigate, aren't you? Why are you here talkin' to me?"

"Mama. I'm retired. I don't have any jurisdiction here."

"That's exactly right." A male voice boomed from behind PC, "We don't need private citizens meddling in police affairs."

"Bah!" Rose spat. "You're just afraid she'll show you up, Elwood."

PC didn't turn around, just kept facing Rose. "Mama, please don't antagonize the Chief. He's got an investigation to supervise. Let him do his job."

Rose folded her hands into her lap. "Harrumph."

Wilson's footsteps echoed behind her as he headed for the crime scene.

PC sat down and reached out to take her mother's hand. "I got over Elwood Wilson forty years ago. You need to let it go."

"He stood you up the night of the Homecoming dance to go play pool with his cousin. And then when you needed him most…"

"Mama, going to that dance would not have stopped Daddy from getting killed. Woody and I, we'd been fighting the whole week before, don't you remember? That's not a shoulder I would have wanted to cry on. Some things… just aren't meant to be."

"He could have had the decency to come to the funeral."

"You're right. He probably should have. But I'm glad he didn't."

PC picked up one of the Thursday night programs from the empty chair next to her and used it as a fan. "I'm roasting."

"They do keep it warm in here."

PC watched as two officers pulled individuals aside to get their statements. She pinched the bridge of her nose and sighed.

"What's wrong?"

"They aren't separating their witnesses. Even if they aren't hiding anything, they'll feed off each other to make their stories more alike, although they thought they saw something different."

"Go tell them that!"

"No. Not my investigation."

"Ha. You just want to see him screw up, don't you?"

Perhaps a little. "Of course not, Mama."

The officers were now speaking with Reverend Deen. The dim fluorescent lighting glinted off his dove-grey suit. His left hand mostly rested against his belly, while he gestured broadly with his right. *Shiny suits. Is that what's in this year?* PC pulled the edge of her collar up and down, trying to get some airflow into her shirt.

Rose cleared her throat. "I wonder where Victoria is? She usually comes to the Thursday night services."

"Victoria?"

"Used to be Victoria Simon. She's the Reverend's wife."

The cheerleader who got Heather Micah's sloppy seconds. "I sort of remember her. Tall blonde?"

"Well, she's a redhead now."

"Ms. Brazwell? Come on, sweetie. That's not your room." PC turned toward the sound of the voice. A nurse was assisting the woman who had found the body. *Of course! She was the wanderer from when I came here to scope it out for Mama.*

A clatter, then some shouting and sounds of a struggle came from outside. All eyes focused on the door, and quiet settled on the remaining witnesses. Time stretched.

The door opened and two officers dragged in a handcuffed man in white scrubs.

"Hey Chief! We found him hiding outside by the dumpsters."

As they got closer, the man looked up, his face a little worse for wear.

Rose gasped. "Rocky?"

Chapter 6

"I DIDN'T DO anything!" Rocky shouted.

The officers stopped dragging him and stood still.

Chief Wilson stepped toward the trio. One of the officers showed something small to his boss, then Wilson spoke quietly to him. The officer headed toward the room where Heather had been found.

Wilson turned his attention back to PC's brother. "Seems curious, you hiding out behind the dumpster if you didn't do anything."

Rocky dropped his head and looked at the floor. "I work here."

PC coughed. *What? When did that happen? Daisy had said no one knew where he was.*

"What did you say?" the Chief got closer.

Rocky raised his head, eyes fierce. "I. Work. Here. I got a job a couple of days ago as a… janitor. I wasn't expectin' Mama to come here, so when I saw her getting dropped off, I took out the trash and just stayed outside. Thought I'd have a smoke."

That explains it. I saw Rocky when I parked the car. Not a 'possum.

The Chief squinted. "Why did you do it?"

"I was embarrassed. I didn't want my mama and my sister to see me like this. I needed some time to get my… act together."

"Don't play dumb with me. You know what I'm talking about."

"Takin' a cigarette break at work is not illegal."

"But murder is."

Rocky's brow furrowed. "What?"

The officer returned from the death scene and dropped something into Wilson's hand before whispering in his ear.

Wilson glanced at PC before he turned his attention back to Rocky. "I'm going to give you a scenario, and you tell me if I'm wrong. You're broke. Because bums are always broke. You got this job, maybe hoping you could steal drugs to sell. Or use yourself. But then you saw Heather Micah come in."

Rocky's cheeks flushed, and he looked like he could cut Wilson in two with his eyes. His jaw clenched and unclenched, but he stayed silent.

"Now this lady is known to have money and was wearing expensive jewelry. You thought you'd take a shortcut and rob her. But she fought back, and you killed her. Does that sound about right?"

"You are fricken crazy. Always have been." He looked to PC and Rose for help.

PC stood and came closer. "You got any evidence for this remarkable story?"

Wilson triumphantly raised an earring. "They found this on him when he was taken into custody. My officer checked, and it matches the one Ms. Micah is still wearing."

"I found it! It was on the floor, under one of the nurse's carts, when I was sweeping up."

PC glared at Wilson. "So you're saying he killed her in a robbery attempt, but failed to take anything but one earring? Do pawn shops pay top dollar for unmatched jewelry around here? Why didn't he take the Rolex watch off her wrist?"

Wilson's face darkened. "I'm taking him back to the station for further questioning."

"I'll be along soon with his attorney." She turned to her brother. "Rocky, I believe you. But keep your mouth shut. I mean it. See you soon."

The two officers marched Rocky out the door.

PC fumed. "The DA's going to laugh you out of his office, and you know it. You don't have a shred of solid evidence to charge my brother. Don't make this personal. If you have a problem with me, you take it up with me."

Wilson's dark eyes were inscrutable. They bored into PC like angry carpenter bees before he turned and strode down the corridor.

PC called her Uncle Raymond, who was the only attorney she knew in Possumwood, and asked him to meet her at the police station. She only had to wait five minutes before he arrived. They walked in together and found Rocky sitting in the lobby, drinking a cup of coffee. PC noticed a Band-Aid on the back of his hand and wondered if it had been there earlier.

"That was a short interrogation." PC looked around the lobby suspiciously.

"Yeah. I sat in there for like five minutes, then that young cop, Asian guy, came in and asked me what happened. I told him my day from start to finish. Never saw Heather Micah, didn't even know she was in town. Then he thanked me for stopping by and told me I was free to go."

"That's a good thing," Raymond said. "Because I mostly handle family law clients–I'm not a criminal defense attorney. But I can recommend a couple of them for you to call in the morning."

Rocky extended his hand, and his uncle took it. "Thanks, Uncle Raymond. I really 'preciate you comin' out."

"Of course. Of course. I'm going to get back to my dinner now. You know how your Aunt Camelia is about mealtimes."

They headed out toward the parking lot.

PC chuckled. "We can always go to the truck stop, if you don't think you'll make it back before the dinner time window closes."

"That would be even worse!" He leaned over and kissed PC on the cheek. "I'll give you a call in the morning."

Rocky opened the door of PC's car and got in. She frowned. *Did I forget to lock it?* In the driver's seat was a burgundy three-ring binder.

She picked it up and opened it. It was a photocopied version of her father's murder book. Xeroxed police reports. Grainy crime scene photos. A few witness statements. Her fingers turned to ice, and she shivered. She'd seen countless crime scenes. But it was different when it was someone she knew.

"What's that?" Rocky asked.

"Nothing." PC pitched the book into the back seat. Too many questions, not enough answers. "When did you get back into town, Rocky? And why didn't you say anything?"

"I heard Daisy was trying to get a hold of me. Then I found out why. I wanted to help. But I'm not much use to anybody. I thought if I could get a job, I could have a chance to get myself together. But employers aren't exactly clamoring for fifty-year-old high school dropouts. It took me a couple a weeks to find the gig at the nursing home. Guess I'll probably get fired from that, now that I'm accused of killin' Heather."

"I'm sorry, Rocky. But you might be wrong. I don't think Azalea Manor is having to turn away throngs of custodian job applicants. Show up at your next shift and see what happens."

"I hope you're right. But Woody's always had a grudge against me. If there's any chance he can pin this on me, he will."

"I won't let that happen."

"And how's that gonna work?"

PC backed out of the parking space and pulled into the street. It took a few minutes for her to organize her thoughts.

"Rocky, when Daddy died, and they didn't catch the killer, there was nothing I could do about it. I was sixteen. When New Year's rolled around a couple of months later, I made the last resolution I will ever make. I resolved that I would catch every killer I could and put them in a cage. That's why I became a cop. If Possumwood PD can't get to the bottom of this," she swallowed hard. "I will."

Rocky snorted. "And how do you know I'm not the killer?"

"I don't. But I know you. And the current evidence doesn't support you being the killer."

"Current evidence. So you're not entirely convinced."

"Did you kill her?"

"No."

I believe you. Don't prove me wrong. I don't want to go there, but I will, if that's where the evidence leads. PC didn't want to think about that.

"Rocky, I understand how hard it was on you to lose Daddy. You were so close. I think he'd be proud of you for working to get your life back on track. I'll do everything in my power to help you. You know that."

He grunted.

Noncommittal. As usual. What else was there to say?

PC pulled into Rose's driveway and cut the engine. She opened the door, giving a surreptitious peek at the binder via the rearview mirror. Who'd put it in her car, and why? It was the last thing she wanted her mother to see, so she'd come back for it later, when she took Cordite out for his evening potty break.

Rose was sitting in the living room, waiting. She struggled to her feet, and Rocky scooped her up in his arms. Her mother hadn't looked so frail before. Or maybe PC just hadn't wanted to see it.

"I'll go make dinner."

PC pulled out a stock pot and filled it with water for pasta. As it heated, she chopped mushrooms and broccoli.

Who left the murder book in my car?

Woody? Seems unlikely. He wouldn't do anything to encourage me to stay in Possumwood or get involved with the police. Would he?

She added a wilting zucchini to the pile of chopped veggies.

Tran? He'd asked if I'd be willing to help with the Micah case. Was he trying to sweeten the pot? He said he'd researched me, so it wouldn't be too hard to connect murdered Trey Donovan to hometown girl Sergeant PC Donovan.

An unsub? If it wasn't Woody or Tran, it had to be someone else, an unknown subject. But why?

Who stands to gain from giving me that file?

Poor Cordite was squirming by the time Rose and Rocky finally decamped to bed. PC picked up her car keys, a festive Christmas-themed dog poop bag, and snapped the leash onto the dog's collar. He barely made it out to the grass, lifting his leg on the large azalea bush that grew by the front porch steps.

"I won't tell Mama if you don't."

The terrier mix trotted slightly ahead as she walked around the block. They were more than halfway through before he paused to make a deposit.

"Finally."

They jogged the rest of the way back to PC's car, where she retrieved the notebook, then slipped in through the garage to leave the gaudy "present" in the outside trash. She briefly wondered if she should dust the binder for prints, but since she didn't have a way to run them through AFIS these days, it would be pointless.

PC got ready to turn in and settled into her bed with the murder book. Cordite jumped up and snuggled next to her. PC scratched his ears, and his tail thumped lightly on the covers.

What is inside? She took a deep breath before opening the binder. The first pages revealed some grainy, black-and-white stills from the security camera footage of the person who'd robbed the convenience store and shot Trey Donovan. The subject was wearing a hat with a hoodie pulled up over it. Gloves. Oversized jacket. Jeans. Tall, probably male, but could have been either, really. The camera was from back in the days of actual video tape. Not great resolution to begin with, and the same tapes were typically recorded and rerecorded until the picture was a staticky mess.

According to the initial incident report. A customer–the high school principal–had come in at 11:45 to buy some beer before the store closed at midnight. He found PC's father on the floor behind the counter and called police. No one had seen or heard anything. As bad as the video was, it seemed to back up the witness' story. He was not as tall as the shooter, and he had a rock-solid alibi–he'd been chaperoning the Homecoming dance.

The follow-up reports noted that rewards had been offered and neighborhoods had been canvassed. Not a single clue had turned up. The prevailing theory was that the robber was someone passing through town who stopped to grab some fast cash at a vulnerable store.

PC studied the pictures some more.

Is that blob in the window a reflection? Could be the killer's face.

It was a long shot. Longer than long, given the terrible resolution. But there was the slimmest of chances that her friend Jack at

NASA might be able to clean it up. She'd worked with him a few times before, and he could just about perform miracles.

She'd call him first thing in the morning.

The droning of the TV kept PC awake. At least that's what she told herself. She got up and padded into the living room.

Her brother flicked aimlessly through the channels.

"Hey, Rocky. You doing okay?"

He shrugged. "You think they believe me?"

"They don't have any evidence that you did anything."

"But you believe me, right?" His voice pitched upward.

"Of course." *Unless evidence turns up to prove me wrong.* "Why don't you get some sleep? You've got work early tomorrow."

Rocky snorted. "You really think I still have a job?"

"I guess we'll find out in the morning."

Chapter 7

"I WAS WONDERING if you'd come back." Durelle Fennec gave Rocky a hard stare from behind her desk.

He looked at the floor. "Yes, ma'am. I'm sorry for all the trouble. But I didn't do anything. I didn't kill her."

Fennec's gaze was inscrutable behind her hooded eyes. PC couldn't tell if the director was mad at Rocky, or mad because his arrest had left her short a janitor. Could be she was just mad at life in general.

"Well, what are you waiting for? Get to work."

"Thank you, ma'am!"

"Go."

Rocky scurried out of the office.

"What time is he off? I'll need to pick him up. Today, anyway." *Did Rocky even have a driver's license?*

Fennec nodded. "He usually works 'til six or seven. Sometimes later–depends on what's going on. He had been sleeping here, in empty beds, as they came available."

"Thank you, for giving Rocky a chance. That means a lot to me."

Her lips squeezed into a tight smile, but it didn't reach Fennec's eyes. "You gotta give people a chance." Her gaze paused on a framed picture on her desk. "I wish someone had given my mama one. But they never did."

"I'm sorry to hear that."

PC could feel a story burgeoning on the other woman's lips. Like a killer about to confess. Fennec picked absently at an oddly round scab on her right arm.

"She used to have a job. A good job. When I was in junior high, we had a nice car, good clothes, there was always food in the house." She shook her heavy head.

PC waited for her to continue.

At last, she did. "She didn't take that money. They called her a thief. They didn't know her at all. She'd never steal so much as a dime."

"Mmm."

Fennec took a long drag on her coffee cup. "They couldn't prove a thing. There was not a shred of evidence against her. Nothing. But they fired her anyway. We lost the house. The car. Had to go live with my grandmother."

PC's ears pricked up. "When was this?"

"Long time ago. Almost forty years. Nobody'd give her a chance to prove her worth. She was called 'thief' in the newspaper, and most people believed it. That's why I give people a second chance. A third chance and a fourth chance if they need it."

"That's very commendable of you, Ms. Fennec. I'm so sorry that happened to your mother. Who fired her?"

"Possumwood High School. She was a secretary in the business office."

"I'm sure your mother was innocent. I mean that. But if you're the one who handles the money, and some of it goes missing, it doesn't look so good."

"Believe me, I'm aware of that. But it wasn't her job to make the bank runs. Ever. Except that one day, when her manager was sick. He'd caught a cold after being soaked too many times in the dunk tank at the band carnival. At least that's what he told people.

Mama and I went over this so many times over the years, trying to figure out who took the money so we could clear her name. Never did, though. All of this because of that horrible girl."

"What girl?"

"The one that lied and told them she saw Mama hide a bag of something under the seat of her car when she made the bank run. I'm glad she got what was coming to her."

"You mean… Heather Micah?"

"Yes."

Interesting. Very interesting. "That seems weird that a high school student would randomly accuse an adult of a crime. Any idea why she'd do that?"

Fennec took another sip of coffee. "I know exactly why."

PC pricked up her ears. "Oh?"

"Mama caught her getting into her car. It was just after lunch–Heather was cutting class. She begged Mama not to turn her in, but she did. Heather claimed she was getting a textbook out of the back seat. Couldn't prove she wasn't." Fennec shrugged.

"That's vindictive with a capital V."

Fennec just nodded.

"I'm sorry to hear about your mother. You have a good day, okay? I'll come for Rocky around six."

Fennec waved PC out of her office.

Mama's menagerie was going to get vocal about breakfast soon, so she hurried home to tend to the critters. A shower and a trip to the post office was in order after that.

After PC dropped the photograph in the mail to Jack, she took a short walk around the town square, courthouse side, to stretch her legs.

It was one of those stellar winter days that is the whole reason for putting up with the brutal southern summer. The air was crisp at around 60°, the sun was bright, and the sky was a deep cerulean, streaked with a few wispy cirrus clouds. There was just enough breeze to carry the scent of distant snow, but not so much that she needed a jacket.

The day would have been perfect, if she'd been able to get the burgundy notebook out of her mind. Who had left it for her? Why? She didn't know any more today than she had the night her father had been struck down in cold blood. Or was there something she was missing? Something the person who'd left it saw, but she didn't.

She had to stop short to avoid crashing into an older couple who had just opened a door in front of her. He carried a large, paper-wrapped object, and she tucked one hand into the crook of his arm. They looked like they'd just won the lottery. They smiled at each other and walked away from PC, laughing and chattering. Very Hallmark Channel.

She wondered if she and Mike would have been like that at this stage in life. If he hadn't been killed by that damn drunk driver weeks before the wedding. She wore the ring he gave her for almost a year after the funeral. It was too hard, too final, to take it off for a long time.

She sighed. The splendid day had taken a somber turn. She hated being ambushed by history.

"Are you going to stand out there all day, or are you coming in?"

Drew Berlusconi held the door to *The Best Little Art Gallery in Texas* open for her.

His grin was enough to scatter the dark clouds that had gathered over her. She scrambled for an excuse to be there as she crossed the threshold into the warm gallery.

"That painting of the chrysanthemum by Lin Youn–I was thinking... I might buy it for my mom. Lin's her next-door neighbor."

"Of course!"

He led her to the painting. Water drops glistened on peach-colored flower petals that floated above green leaves and stems. She almost reached out to blot the water from the canvas, the droplets looked so real. It was a steal at $50.

"All the enjoyment of fresh flowers, none of the hassle." His lips parted in a half-smile.

"That's one way to look at it."

Drew took the painting down from its easel, and PC followed him back to the front, where he got out a roll of brown paper.

"Did you want a frame?"

"It doesn't come with one?"

He rummaged around behind the counter for a moment. "How about this one? I think the mahogany will be a great contrast for the peach and orange in the painting."

It looked expensive. She was afraid to ask how much, but wondered how tacky it would be to make a run to one of the craft chain stores for a cheaper one.

"It's on me."

Am I that transparent? "Thank you so much! You don't have to do that."

Drew shrugged. "My pleasure."

PC eyed a long scratch that started just below Drew's jaw and disappeared under his collar. "I hope the other guy looks worse."

He looked up, confused.

"Looks like someone tried to go for your jugular."

His hand rose to his throat. "Oh, that. I was unblocking the pump of the fountain in my courtyard last night and had a disagreement with the screwdriver."

"Oh. Glad it's nothing serious."

As he prepared the painting, PC looked at the pictures near the front. One was a huge rendition of a woman in a canoe in the middle of a very large lake at night. White horses splashed in the shallows to her left. *Wasn't that the one Heather Micah commented on that made Drew angry? What was the name of the artist she suggested? Bertoli? Bucatini?*

PC moved closer to see if she could make out the signature. She thought she spotted it but couldn't tell if it was writing or just errant brush strokes. *Deen? Doan? The name Heather used was much longer... Beltracchi! That's what she'd said, and that's what seemed to be the final straw that made Drew call the cops.*

"So, is this one a local talent? Didn't Heather say it was a Beltracchi?"

"Certainly not!" The vehemence of Drew's words made PC jump. "That is an original Patrick Daun."

"Okay."

Drew slapped tape onto the brown paper, then paused to glare at PC "You don't know who Wolfgang Beltracchi is, do you?" It was more of a statement than a question.

"No."

"He's a notorious art forger. Extraordinarily talented, embarrassed a lot of art authenticators. Made millions before he was sent to prison. There was a couple, old money art collectors, here in the gallery on Wednesday night, who were looking for an investment quality piece. They were interested in the Daun until *that woman* started insinuating it was a forgery."

Drew finished wrapping, so PC took out her wallet and handed him her Visa. She looked at the Daun. "How much—"

The sleigh bells on the door jingled as a trio of hipsters came into the gallery.

"Good afternoon, gentlemen." He handed PC her credit card. "If you'd like to meet me for dinner at *Truffles!*, we could discuss it further."

"To discuss art?" PC gave him a coy smile. "What time?"

"Eight?"

"See you then."

Rocky got out of the car. "Thanks for the ride."

"Sure."

PC sat in her mother's driveway for a few minutes before she went inside, using her phone to look for paintings by Patrick Daun. A Daun original could go for upwards of seven figures. How on earth had a small-town art dealer managed to end up with one? This was going to be an amazing story. But would it be fiction? The way he'd reacted when she'd mentioned Beltracchi made that seem unlikely.

She found herself humming as she carried the wrapped painting into her mother's house. Rose was sitting in her recliner. The TV was on, but she didn't seem to be paying much attention to it.

"Mama, I brought you something."

Rose looked up, her eyes unfocused. "What ish it?"

PC leaned the artwork against the wall and moved to her mother's side. "Mama, are you alright? Your eyes are awfully red."

Rose gave her a lop-sided smile.

"Mama, raise your arms."

One arm flopped over her head, and the other jutted straight out from her shoulder. Then she dissolved into fits of giggling.

Oh, god. I think she's had a stroke.

Chapter 8

PC FUMBLED FOR her phone. "I'm going to call an ambulance."

Rocky came into the living room from the kitchen. "An ambulance? Why?" His brow furrowed. "Mama, you seen those brownies that were sittin' on the table?"

Rose started laughing so hard PC wondered if she'd be able to breathe.

"Justice and Lin came over, so we et 'em."

Rocky's jaw went slack. "Mama! You didn't!"

"Who cares about your stupid brownies? I've got to get her to the hospital!"

Rocky's brow furrowed. "Why?"

"Why? Because I think she's had a stroke." PC woke her phone.

Her brother put a hand over hers to stop her. "She's fine."

"What do you mean, she's fine? Look at her!"

Rose cackled to herself in the recliner.

"Those brownies were, um, full of herbs."

PC blinked several times. "Herbs?"

Rocky gestured with his hands. "You know. *Herbs.*"

"You fed my mother and her friends space cakes?"

He held his hands up, palms towards his sister. "I didn't feed it to them. They did that themselves. They didn't even leave me any."

PC tucked her hands into her armpits to keep herself from slapping her brother. "Are you selling drugs?"

"What? Of course not!" Rocky deflated. "A friend. In Colorado. I didn't buy them. She just sent them to me–she's trying out some new recipes."

"You do realize marijuana is not currently legal in Texas, right? Do. Not. Let people mail you drugs here. If Woody catches wind of this, he's going to throw both of us under the jail."

Rocky bowed his head.

PC was unmoved. "You stay here with Mama and watch her. Don't move. Just keep an eye on her and make sure she's okay. I'm going to check on the other two."

The detective trotted across the yard to the Youn's house. Lin was sitting in the front porch swing with a bag of chips. Her husband stood in the doorway, behind the screen.

"Hey, Lin, Mr. Youn. I just, uh, found out the brownies my mother served this afternoon, were, uh, spiked."

Mr. Youn nodded, his lips pursing.

"I'm really sorry. Mama didn't know. Lin should be fine. Just, uh, don't let her drive."

Justice yawned deeply as she opened the door for PC. "Come in, hon." The older woman sat on the divan.

PC swallowed. "I just wanted to come by and tell you, when Mama served you those brownies, she didn't know they were, um, adulterated."

Justice yawned again and stretched out. "Mmmm. Okay."

"I needed to make sure you were alright, let you know about…"

Rose's friend had nodded off. PC covered her with the ripple crochet afghan that was draped across the chair and left.

What am I going to do with Rocky? I'll have to worry about that after dinner, when I find out just how many reasons Drew Berlusconi had to want Heather Micah dead.

Truffles! was a lot fancier than PC had expected. She forced a smile to challenge the disapproving look of the Maitre d' as his eyes rolled coldly over her polo shirt and slacks. She did own a dress, but it was back at her house in Houston. The last thing she expected when she came to Possumwood was a fine-dining dinner date.

But here she was, being seated across from Drew, who had come prepared in a blue sport coat and van Gogh *Starry Night* print tie.

A silent young woman in a starched white shirt and dark purple tie filled their water glasses and flitted away before PC could say, "Thank you."

She wasn't sure if Drew had assumed he was paying the tab, but she was planning on going Dutch. There were no misunderstandings that way.

PC picked up the menu and coughed from sticker shock. Rose had told her it was fine dining, but $35+ for a steak seemed steep, given how far they were out in the sticks. She found a more budget-friendly salad for $16. She considered a baked potato on the side but couldn't bring herself to pay 10 bucks for a spud she could buy in the grocery store for less than a dollar.

Almost as soon as she closed her menu, a waiter in a dark purple waistcoat and matching tie appeared at their table, as if summoned by magic.

"Madame?"

"I'll have the wild field greens with berries and avocado salad, please."

"Excellent choice, madame. And you, sir?"

"The salmon Pontchartrain, please. Are you sure the salad is enough, PC?"

"I like a light dinner."

The waiter collected the menus. "That will be the wild field greens salad for madame, and the salmon Pontchartrain for monsieur. Very good." He melted away as quickly as he'd arrived. The same woman who'd brought them water swept by, leaving a plate of rolls with molded herb butter in her wake.

PC was starving, but she daintily picked up a roll, split and buttered it, then set it on her bread plate. "Mama had said there was fine dining in Possumwood, but I didn't actually believe her."

"Yes." Drew got his own bread. "It's very continental. Michele Jorgensen is from Switzerland."

"Is she the owner?"

"She and her husband, Felix."

Felix Jorgensen. That name seemed familiar... Yes. She'd known *of* Felix in high school, but he'd been several grades below her, and they'd had no friends in common.

"So, tell me more about the Daun you have in your gallery. I looked him up–that seems incredible that you'd have one."

The sommelier showed up with the wine list.

PC held up her hands. "No, thank you."

Disappointment flickered across Drew's face, but he also refused.

The wine steward inclined his head slightly. "Enjoy your meal." He moved smoothly to another table.

Drew took a sip of his water. "Now, where were we?"

"The Daun."

"Now that's a story. My grandmother used to own an apartment building in New York City. Patrick Daun's aunt lived there, and when he first immigrated to the US, he stayed with her. When the aunt died, her relatives picked through the apartment for anything they thought was valuable and left the rest for maintenance to dispose of. One of the things they left behind was one of Daun's very early works. He hadn't become famous yet. It's a little bit like if you look at van Gogh–*The Potato Eaters* differs vastly from *Starry Night*." He ran his fingers over his tie, as if he'd brought it specifically for show-and-tell. "Anyway, my grandmother liked the painting and hung it up in her living room. I don't remember how many years it was there before she died. When I was helping my parents clean out her house, I realized what it was and brought it home with me. And that's how it came to be in my gallery."

"Does Patrick Daun know you have it?"

"Sure! He and his lawyer came to challenge the authenticity, but when he saw it, he remembered the painting. Since it had been thrown out with the trash, he had no claim to it. He laughed and thanked me for reminding him of his kind auntie. He even autographed the certificate of authenticity."

PC leaned forward. "Would you think I'm crass if I asked you how much it was worth?"

Drew's eyes sparkled. "Of course not! I'm asking 600, but it may fetch more at auction."

"Six hundred dollars sounds like a steal. I might buy it myself." PC finally took a bite of her bread.

"Six hundred *thousand* dollars."

She took a drink of water to wash down the roll that had suddenly stuck in her throat. "Maybe not."

A lot of people have been killed for a lot less money.

Drew raised his hand to wave at someone. "Felix!"

A tall man–PC guesstimated just under six and a half feet–dressed in an apron and puffy chef's hat came to their table. His dishwater blond beard and mustache were trimmed close against his pink cheeks.

"Drew. Who is your lovely companion?"

Drew stood up. PC felt awkward just sitting there, so she got to her feet as well.

"Felix Jorgensen, this is PC Donovan. PC, Felix. She's Rose Donovan's daughter."

PC extended her hand and Felix took it in both of his. "I thought you looked familiar. You went to Possumwood High, didn't you?"

"Go, Panthers."

Felix squeezed her hand harder. "Your brother, he performed a community service."

PC bristled. "I beg your pardon?"

"That Heather Micah," Felix pursed his lips and shook his head. "I can't believe she had the gall to come into my restaurant."

She forced her arm to relax, and as soon as his grip loosened, PC extracted her hand from Felix's grasp. "What makes you say that?"

Over Jorgensen's shoulder, she could see Drew's eyes narrow. *Poor guy. He surely hadn't planned on an evening of story time with Felix. Probably regretting waving him over, now.*

Jorgensen scowled and shook his head. "I guess you'd already left town. She accused my brother, Robert, of assaulting her. He got sent to prison." His hand knotted into a fist and pounded the air. "He was later exonerated, but he lost almost ten years of his life. He was never the same- the smart, happy teenager that got locked up came out a bitter, hardened man. When she came in here with that smirk on her face, I threw that piece of trash out, told her never to come back. I'm not at all sorry she's dead. I'm surprised someone hadn't killed her sooner."

Was there anyone, besides Daisy, who didn't hate Heather?

"I can understand that. Someone perhaps did a community service, but it wasn't my brother."

"No? I heard they arrested him."

"They took him downtown to ask him some questions. But they had no evidence against him. Because he's innocent. They released him. I picked him up from the police station myself."

"If he didn't do it, I'm glad *someone* did. It was a long time coming. I have to get back to the kitchen."

PC and Drew sat back down.

She took a sip of water. "I have the vaguest recollection of Mama talking about this. Heather left no earth unscorched."

"Seems like quite a piece of work. I hadn't realized you grew up around here. Should have guessed, though."

"I did… grow up here." PC racked her brain for other topics than her personal ancient history.

"You must know everybody, then."

"Not really. I know a number of people in Possumwood, true. But some have left, and others have moved in since I lived here." PC shrugged. "It was a long time ago. Hey, do you get into town–Houston–much? Museum of Fine Art is hosting an Impressionists exhibition in a couple of weeks."

"I saw that. Are you fond of Impressionists?"

"Of course, the classic masters are excellent, but there are some contemporary artists I like as well."

Drew nodded. He opened his mouth as if to say something, but the waiter arrived with the food. He set a hot plate in front of Drew, then placed a mixing bowl full of greens, avocado, fresh berries, dried cranberries, and candied walnuts before PC.

That's a lot of roughage.

"Cheese, madame?"

"Just a little."

The grater spun and parmesan snowed down on the mountain of vegetation.

"That's good. Thanks.

She poured in a little of the dressing and used both her fork and spoon to mix the salad components together.

Light glinting off the beveled glass of the front door caught PC's eye and she glanced up.

Stepping into *Truffles!* in their conspicuously expensive designer clothes were none other than the Reverend Joshua Deen and his lovely wife, Victoria.

Chapter 9

PC CHEWED A mouthful of some miscellaneous leafy greens and watched as surreptitiously as she could. She didn't want Drew to feel neglected and turn his head to see what she was looking at.

Victoria was still tall, still leggy and thin. Probably spent hours in the gym. Her now bright chestnut hair curled down to her shoulder blades and was held out of her face with a small, bejeweled clasp. Perhaps the soft lighting cast shadows on her face, but she looked peaked.

"How is Rose doing by the way?"

PC swallowed the vegetation down. "Fine. She's still using a cane, but the doctor said she'd be fully healed in a couple of months. Maybe less."

A hostess led the Deens to the table behind Drew. PC looked down, hoping not to be noticed. The reverend–her former classmate–would probably remember her, but she doubted Victoria would–she was younger, and, like Felix, they never ran in the same circles.

Joshua pulled out his chair and started to take his jacket off. But then he winced, put his hand over his heart, and left the coat on. They both sat down, and PC was thrilled that they were sitting so that she could see each of them in profile, but neither was looking directly at her.

"I'm glad to hear she's doing well." Drew took a sip of his water. "Have you given any more thought to coming to the Saturday workshop? One of our local artists is teaching about Chinese brush painting?"

PC speared an avocado slice and a couple of blueberries. "What's the difference, really, between Chinese brush painting and regular watercolor? Not that I'm an expert, by any stretch."

Behind them, a chair scraped across wood.

"But Vicki—" Joshua Deen's words were cut short.

"I'm *going* to the ladies' room." Victoria snatched her small handbag from the back of the chair and strode across the dining area, heels clicking on the hardwood floor with an angry tsk, tsk, tsk.

Drew cleared his throat. "The Chinese watercolors use quite different pigments than Western style ones. They're designed to be applied to rice paper, whereas the other type really should be on watercolor paper."

He carried on with a dissertation about the virtues of various pigments, while PC watched the reverend. His left hand remained stabilized on the table while he awkwardly dug his cell phone out of his pocket. He set it next to his plate and began pecking at the keyboard with the fingers of his right hand.

Drew had moved on to the history of rice paper. Ordinarily, PC might have been interested–she had taken that art history continuing ed class at Rice University, after all–but right now, her focus was on the reverend's peculiar behavior.

"Really? I can't even go wash my hands without you texting some floozy?" Vicki stood by her chair, glaring at her husband. A few other people had turned to look, but she didn't seem to care.

"Of course not, darling! Please sit down. I was just checking my index funds." Friendly words, but fake smile and hard eyes.

"… the nineteenth-century Europeans called it rice paper, but it wasn't really made from rice. Are you familiar with Egyptian papyrus?"

"Mmhm."

Vicki sat, but her eyes burned with fury.

"… and they boiled the branches until the bark slipped off…"

"I don't know why you're mad at me. I was looking for you–if you'd just replied to my texts, none of this would have happened." Vicki glugged red wine.

"… and once it's processed, some of it is dyed to make paper flowers. But the rest…"

"Darling. Calm down. I was only wondering where you were when everybody else was at the nursing home getting ready for the show."

She slammed the goblet down, sloshing half of it out. Merlot spread like a bloodstain on the white tablecloth. "What are you trying to say?"

He gestured for her to keep her voice down. "I was busy with the setup and didn't hear the phone. That's all."

"And you expect me to believe that? I know she was texting you."

Conversations lulled as other diners rubbernecked at the reverend's train wreck of a dinner.

"… and mulberry paper was also common for calligraphy. The silkworms don't like mature mulberry leaves, so they had to…"

"Victoria! You're attracting attention," Joshua hissed through clenched teeth.

"Isn't that what you want from your women? You dated Heather so you could have the head cheerleader dangling off your arm like some-some-designer handbag!"

PC could see Joshua shift into damage control mode. He allowed his shoulders to slump and pasted on an aggrieved half-smile on his thin lips. Loudly, in his preacher's voice, he said, "Darling, I can see how upset you are. It was very shocking to lose your best friend so suddenly."

"Heather Micah was nobody's friend." Vicki snatched her purse from the chair and stormed out.

Joshua sighed loudly and stood slowly. "Poor dear." He shook his head. "I fear this has all been too much for her."

He dropped his napkin on the table and followed his wife out the front door.

"... and that is how the silk industry fed the art world–fast-growing trees and picky caterpillars."

PC collected some walnuts on her fork. "Huh. I never knew any of that." She glanced at the Deen's now-empty table. *I suspected most of that.*

"There's a quiz later." Drew dabbed at his mouth with the napkin.

"What?"

"Kidding. You weren't really paying attention, anyway."

The detective set down her fork. "I'm sorry. Woody–Chief Wilson–is determined to pin this murder on my brother. Rocky's a lot of things, but he isn't a killer.

He picked up his glass. "I thought you were retired. Are you investigating Heather's murder?"

"No! Of course not."

Drew raised an eyebrow.

"Okay. Not officially. But I'm not going to let them send my brother to jail for something he didn't do. I'm just trying to catch any evidence PPD might overlook, that's all. They don't have a lot of experience in homicide investigations."

He chuckled. "I guess you can take the girl out of the police department, but you can't take the police department out of the girl."

"Maybe not." She stabbed some more leaves and a crouton.

Their purple-vested waiter appeared at the table. "How does everything taste? Is there anything I can get for you?"

"Could we get the check, please? Separate tickets."

"Very good, madame." And he was gone. *Hope Drew didn't need more tea.*

She turned to her companion. "I'm sorry. I've got to go check on Mama. This dinner has been a bit dramatic, and I feel bad that we didn't get to talk all that much. How about after the workshop on Saturday, we go have a coffee?"

His face lit up. "That's an excellent idea. I'm looking forward to it. You know, I would have been happy to buy you a salad."

"I appreciate that. But I'd rather pay my own way. Cuts down on misunderstandings."

PC was thinking about the Deens' public fight, analyzing angry words for clues, when she noticed red and blue lights flashing in her rearview mirror. A glance at the speedometer showed she was actually two mph under the limit.

"Great."

She pulled into the Justice Avenue Baptist Church's parking lot and stopped under one of the tall, dim lights.

There was a tap on her passenger side window, and she saw it was Hiro Tran. She hit the button, and the glass slid down. He leaned inside.

"Evening, Detective."

"Tran. What's up?"

He handed her a manila envelope. "Photos of Heather Micah's personal effects. There are a few interesting things."

"Why are you giving me these?"

Tran considered for a few moments. "Mind if I sit down?"

PC unlocked the door.

He got in and gave a glance toward the road. "We don't get very many homicides. The few we do have, there's usually a bar full of witnesses involved. I could use your help."

And I could stand to keep track of where this investigation is going.

PC pulled out the prints. The first was of Heather's suitcase, a carry-on sized roller bag.

"Looks like she was traveling light."

A snapshot of the closet showed three dresses hanging there, with one pair of expensive shoes on the floor. The bathroom counter held some cosmetics and face cream, as well as a toothbrush and travel-sized toothpaste.

The next picture showed an apartment eviction notice, and another was of a receipt from a storage unit.

Hiro tapped the photo. "Those looked like they'd been folded up and stuck in her luggage in a hurry. What if she got a cab straight from the storage locker to the airport?"

"She gets booted out of her apartment for nonpayment. So, we can infer she's got no money. Her things are in storage, so she either planned to go back to LA or send for them. Her sister doesn't live here anymore, so why did she come to Possumwood?"

"To get a job and make enough money to get her stuff?"

"Then why bring only three outfits? She's not really qualified to do anything, other than act. She'd be better off in Houston, or staying with her sister in Wichita Falls, if that was her plan. Seems like she thought she could come to Possumwood for a few days and go home with some cash."

"Blackmail?"

"Seems like a reasonable guess. Unless she had a chest full of doubloons buried in the woods somewhere. Or a safe deposit box… Did you find a return plane ticket?"

Hiro shook his head. "No, no plane ticket."

"Could have been on her phone. Have you gotten it unlocked?"

"Her phone's missing."

"Of course, it is. Someone that she's called or texted since she got here is probably the person who killed her."

PC pulled out the next photo. It was an old newspaper clipping. The edges of the paper had yellowed. A headline blared at the top of the page:

BAND CARNIVAL EARNINGS DISAPPEAR
SECRETARY FIRED

Durelle Fennec's mother. "Yes. The band had raised a bunch of money for a trip, but when it came time to set it up, there was no money in the account. It had never made it to the bank. They fired the admin who made the bank deposits, but the money never turned up, and she was never charged–no evidence."

Hiro nodded thoughtfully. "Perhaps Heather knew who took the money."

The band theft wasn't front-page news, and the clipping was about a fourth of the news sheet, as if someone had torn it along the creases. Underneath the band story was the continuation of what had definitely been a story from the front page.

SECOND TRAGEDY IN TWO MONTHS STRIKES POSSUMWOOD (cont.)

The second tragedy was Tom Able. The coach of the state-champion winning Possumwood Panthers football team had been killed in a car crash on the way home from the championships. Investigators had speculated that he'd gotten drowsy and run off the road into a tree.

The first tragedy was Trey Donovan. PC's father. He'd been murdered in an armed robbery at the family's convenience store the month before. The night of Homecoming Dance. The clipping was like a punch in the stomach. She ran her hand over her face to try to focus on Heather Micah's demise.

"I wasn't in band, but you can easily track down the people who were. The school should have a copy of the yearbook, or at least they'll have all the student records."

"A lot of those yearbooks are digitized and online now."

"That makes it easy. If the Possumwood Panthers have been scanned."

"Well, we've got a warrant for Heather's phone records, but sometimes that can take a while. I guess I'll look through old yearbooks until they come back."

"Has the Medical Examiner finished the autopsy yet?"

"Report's in there. Cause of death was a broken neck, although she also had blunt force trauma to the back of the head."

"And they did fingernail scrapings and a rape kit?"

"They didn't find anything. I gotta get back on my beat. If anyone asks, you got a warning for a bad taillight."

Who's going to ask? "Thanks for the update."

"How was your date, Primrose?" Rose burst into laughter.

"Fine, Mama."

She glared at her brother, who sat on the couch with his stocking feet propped on the coffee table. Cordite lay next to him. Rocky fed him a piece of popcorn. The dog's tail thumped as he looked at his owner, but he continued loafing.

"How long is she going to be like this? And if you make my dog sick giving him people food, you're cleaning it up."

"Chill, sis. Mama'll be back to her usual self by morning. Cordie and me are just watching some wrasslin'. Why don cha take a load off and hang out?"

"I'm going to have a quick check on the animals. I'll take Cordite out to pee while I'm there." She looked around for the leash.

Rose cackled. "You said pee!"

It was going to be a long night.

Chapter 10

PC HAD JUST stepped out of the shower and was blotting her hair. The beasties were fed, and their pen scooped. Now she was deodorized and could get on with her day.

"Primrose!"

She wrapped her towel around her wet body and ran into the living room. "What is it, Mama? Are you okay?"

"Of course, I am. Just really hungry, and there's not much food in the house. You wanna go get something to eat?"

PC glanced at her FlitBit. "It's only ten. A little early for lunch."

"Would you believe there are places here in town that also serve breakfast? You can call it brunch if that suits you better."

"Fine, Mama. Where do you want to go?"

"I have a hankerin' for *The Brisk Rib*. Best barbecue in town."

Probably the only barbecue in town. "Sure. Give me a few minutes to get dressed. Rocky coming?"

"No. He's working. Took my car."

"Good."

A copper cowbell on the front door clattered as they entered. *The Brisk Rib* had gotten their money's worth from their decorator. The restaurant looked like the inside of an old wooden barn. Rough-hewn posts supported the ceiling, and the ordering queue was fenced in with a split rail barrier. Red and white checked vinyl tablecloths brightened the tables. The place was in the heart of downtown Possumwood, and PC hoped no city employees were also having brunch. At least not a certain Chief of Police, anyway.

"Miss Rose! It's so wonderful to see you." The woman behind the counter waved at them. She looked to be on the young side of middle age and wore a red bandana, Rosie the Riveter style, on her bottle blonde hair.

"Sadie! It's good to see you, too, hon. I'll have my usual, but I don't know what my daughter here wants."

Sadie tapped on the tablet in front of her, then smiled expectantly at PC. A man in a white apron came out of the kitchen carrying a basket of towels.

"Miz Donovan! I heard you were back from the hospital. Glad to see you this morning."

"Oh, thank you, Frank. It's so good to be home. Had to get my barbecue fix!"

"Welcome back!" He grinned and nodded toward PC before going out the side door with the laundry.

Did I go to school with him? He looks vaguely familiar. PC scanned the huge menu on the wall. "I'll have the... Brisk Tater #3."

"Yes, ma'am. Ya'll want drinks?"

"Sure."

Rose hobbled off to find a table. PC paid and took the waxed paper cups to the soda fountain to fill them with iced tea.

Her mother smiled when PC set down the drinks. "I'm so glad Durelle didn't fire Rocky, after all. I always said that girl had a good heart. It's a real shame the owners of that nursing home don't give her nearly enough money to run the place the way it should be."

"It is shabby."

Rose took a sip of her tea and almost spat it out. "What is this?"

"Tea, Mama."

"Go dump this raw tea and get me some sweet tea."

PC picked up her mother's drink and took it back to the beverage station. The cowbell jangled, and she heard Sadie say, "Hey, Chief."

"Hey, Sadie."

Hiding behind the soda machine, the detective filled the cup with sweet tea. *Not now.* She hoped he'd get his order to go. She examined the lids and straws.

Then Woody's voice again. "Mornin', Frank."

"You found the killer yet, Elwood?"

"We're working on that."

"Yeah? Well, you call me as soon as you do. I've already got the parade route planned–just need to get the permit."

"A bit over the top, don't you think?"

"Whoever offed her deserves a medal. Don't look at me like that."

"What she did to Bernadette was awful. I agree with you there. But Heather didn't murder her."

"Maybe not with her own hands. But it's 100% her fault. I've got to go show the delivery truck where to unload. New driver. You catch that killer. I want to shake his hand."

PC returned to the table, her back to Woody. She pretended not to notice he was there.

"Where did you go to get that tea? China?"

"Is there enough ice for you, Mama?"

Rose stabbed at the liquid with a tea spoon. "Looks fine."

PC cast a glance over her shoulder. "What was that was about?"

"What's that?"

"What Frank and Woody were talking about. Bernadette."

Rose toyed with the container of sugar packets. "If I knew anything about her, I've forgotten it."

Have you? Or you just don't want to tell me? "Okay."

Sadie brought their food. PC's spud was a mutant colossus that looked half as big as Cordite. *At least I've got lunch for tomorrow, too. And the next day.* She probed it tentatively with her fork.

Rose grinned over a brisket sandwich. "I've missed this place so much!"

"You know what? You're right, Mama."

Rose paused, a forkful of coleslaw almost to her lips. "About what?"

"Well, Possumwood. It's really changed a lot since I left."

"I told you! We've got all sorts of amenities. Without all the big city traffic."

"Yeah. Seems like a lot of people either stayed here or came back after college and started businesses." *But I can't wait to get out of here.*

"Like Frank Smith. Possumwood wouldn't be the same without the *Brisk Rib*."

I wonder how Tran's doing with those old yearbooks. Are the Possumwood Panthers online? If I can find Frank Smith, maybe I can find Bernadette, or at least, how she died. "I'm sure you're right, Mama."

Rose prattled on about how she would be keeping her resolutions this year. New Year, new you! PC nodded and mumbled the occasional "Mmhum." She was turning over puzzle pieces in her head. Seemed like half the town had a reason to hate Heather Micah–revenge can be a powerful motive. But how many of them had means and opportunity?

Felix Jorgensen had a very public altercation with the victim, but he was working at his restaurant at the time of the murder.

Drew Berlusconi lost a lot of money because of Heather's interference. But there wasn't any evidence that he was ever at the nursing home.

Victoria Deen, who was conspicuously absent from the Thursday night sermon, thought Heather might be trying to hook up with the good reverend. She clearly doesn't trust her husband. Jealousy kills.

Durelle Fennec despised Heather. She was working at Azalea Manor when the murder happened. Motive and opportunity. Did she have the means? It's plausible. Heather died of a broken neck, with blunt force trauma to the back of the head. Could be she fell. After she was shoved.

Frank Smith blamed her for the death of Bernadette. Sister? Girlfriend? Pet? For all I know, she ran over his dog. Accidentally, of course. Need more information.

"Primrose? Honey, are you okay?"

"I'm sorry. What?"

"Don't you like your potato? You've hardly touched it."

PC set her naked fork on the edge of her plate. "It's fine. Just not as hungry as I thought. I'll get a to-go box."

A bottom crust of bread and a pool of coleslaw dressing were all that remained on Rose's plate. PC smiled at the dish. It was good to see her mother getting back to her usual self. The detective got up to ask Sadie for a box and was handed a cardboard container.

"Now, ma'am just so you know, that box's got seeds in it. If you put it out in your flowerbed, you can grow you some basil and stuff."

"How about that? Thanks."

Is this even going to hold that monster spud? She frowned at the potato on her plate. While she was dissecting her leftovers and

Holly Dey

Tetris-ing the pieces into the container, the cowbell clanged, and suddenly Hiro Tran was at their table.

"I saw your car out front and thought you'd want to know—your brother's just been arrested for the murder of Heather Micah."

Chapter 11

"What?" Rose grabbed the edges of the table to steady herself.

PC reached out to touch her mother's hands. "What's going on? Why was *he* arrested?"

Tran sat down in one of the empty chairs. "Two of the victim's hairs were found on his clothes. There were a few drops of blood on the floor–someone tried to wipe them up but missed a spot–that belonged to a male. DNA's not back on it yet. Your brother's hands had several scratches."

"How is the DNA back on the hair, but not the blood?"

"There wasn't a root, but they're trying for mitochondrial DNA. They did a microscopic hair strand comparison to Heather's, though."

"You are aware that's been mostly debunked, right?"

"Not my call."

"So far, everything you have is circumstantial."

"Not everything."

PC shifted in her chair. "Go on."

"Rocky's phone was found under the blanket with Heather's body."

Rose started taking rapid, shallow breaths. "What are you sayin'?"

"Mama, focus on your breathing. You hyperventilating and passing out isn't going to do anybody any good."

She turned to Tran. "You're investigating my brother, but you're feeding me information and asking for my help. Is there something you aren't telling me?"

Tran fiddled with the silverware packet at his seat. "Well…"

Hesitation. You're hiding something, are you? "Do you think the investigation's being botched?"

"I didn't say that."

But you think it. "I'm sure you realize your boss won't be happy if he finds out you've been talking to me about the case."

"I know. I…"

PC's heart nearly broke when she saw tears streaming down her mother's face. "Mama, we're going to do everything we can. It's going to be okay."

Tran looked miserably down at the table. "Mrs. Donovan? When you sold the ShopStop to my grandparents, they were so incredibly grateful for a chance at the American Dream. Bà thought the world of you."

"Your grandmother was a genuinely nice lady. I felt lucky I was able to sell the place so quickly after… what happened."

The plastic tumbler clunked on the table when PC set it down. There would be time for emotions later. Now, they would just get in the way. "Hiro. Thank you for helping. We really appreciate it." *Now go.*

Rose blotted her eyes with her napkin. "I know it looks bad for Rocky, but he didn't do this. Lord knows he's wandered far off the straight and narrow, but a murderer?" She shook her head. "No. That's just not him."

You might be surprised what people are capable of, Mama. PC patted her mother's hands. "If we're going to prove Rocky didn't kill Heather, we need to find out who did. In the meantime, I need you to call Uncle Raymond and get a lawyer over to the jail."

"Durelle." Rose smacked the table with the flat of her hand. "Why don't you just ask her–I'm sure she can tell you where Rocky was that evening."

Tran shook his head. "We tried that, but no one knows where she is."

Very convenient, if you happen to be the killer, Ms. Fennec. "So what you're saying is that someone who had motive, means, and opportunity to kill Heather has skipped town, but you're arresting Rocky, who has absolutely no motive? He could have dropped his phone, or set it down somewhere, and anyone could have picked it up and placed it with the body. Especially someone who wanted to frame him to take the heat off themselves. Were there any fingerprints?"

"Just Rocky's."

"They could have worn gloves. It's a nursing home - people use gloves constantly."

Hiro shook his head slightly. "That may be true, but I don't have any gloves. Only the phone. There are trashcans full of gloves–what would it prove to check them all for DNA? You said yourself that everybody there uses them."

Rose sniffled and got up to make her phone call outside. PC watched her hobble through the double doors and into the pale sun.

"This is the last thing Mama needs while she's trying to recover from her operation."

"I'm sorry. But I thought you'd want to know."

"Thanks. I appreciate it. I'm sorry if it doesn't come out that way."

"Understood. I've got to get back to the station."

Flight is probably the surest sign of guilt. Where did you fly to, Ms. Fennec? PC tapped her thumbs on the steering wheel, a tic she'd developed when deep in thought. She'd just left Rose at the city jail with her Uncle Raymond, in hopes of getting Rocky bailed out of the slammer. But given that he was being held on suspicion of murder, there was a good chance that wouldn't happen. She nearly missed the driveway for Azalea Manor. She had to look around for herself–she didn't trust Woody to do a proper investigation. When the most common crime a department deals with on a regular basis is the high school kids getting drunk under the bridge… they didn't handle many–any–homicides, did they? It wasn't their fault they had no experience. And lucky them.

PC parked and cut the engine. She took a moment to take a few deep breaths and collect herself. The last thing that would help is for angry big sis to go storming in, threatening to kick butt and take names. Her furor had overtaken her dread of hospitals. Still, she needed a pretext, a reason to be there asking questions about Durelle Fennec.

The folder. The one with all the forms that Fennec had given her when she'd toured the place. She could say she lost it, and she needed another one. That would get her into the office and talking to whoever was in charge now.

She eased inside and walked down the hall. At Fennec's office, she knocked on the frame of the open door.

"Excuse me? Ma'am?"

A thin woman, blonde hair pulled severely into a bun, looked up. "Is there something I can help you with?" The beady eyes on either side of her long, pinched nose broadcast suspicion.

"Yes, ma'am. I sure hope so. Can you tell me when Ms. Fennec'll be back?"

"No. I can't."

Can't, or won't? "Well, you see, ma'am, I was here last week for a tour. Ms. Fennec–nice lady–she gave me a folder with some forms in it, but I seem to have misplaced it."

Her lips pursed. "And you want another one?"

PC looked at the floor. "Yes, ma'am. It's weird. I spoke with Ms. Fennec just this morning."

The woman's eyebrow arched.

"On the phone. I called about the forms."

She opened a drawer and pulled a manila envelope off a stack of identical envelopes. "She's not here now."

So much for building a rapport. She won't even tell me her name.

"Would you mind showing me the available rooms? I'd like to see them again before I decide."

The Woman With No Name stood up, then took a clipboard that was hanging on the wall. "This way." She paused for a moment to look at the map in her hand. "Is your relative ambulatory? There's no more space for dementia patients. Ms. Fennec should have told you that."

"She did, ma'am. Yes. And yes, my mother can walk."

No Name led PC down the hall. At the one sealed with crime scene tape, she paused. "Is that where…?"

"There was a murder there. I don't know much about it. At least the room was empty at the time. One patient was in the hospital, and the other, God rest her soul, had just passed that morning before. Her family hadn't had time to get her things boxed up, and now, all those stuffed animals are just sitting there. I think they'd wanted some for the funeral. Sad."

A female voice came from down the hall. "Mrs. Brazwell. That's not your room, sweetie."

PC clenched her jaw to suppress a grin. "Yes, ma'am." She was pretty sure she knew how Rocky's phone got into the bed. "Thank you for the tour, ma'am. And the forms. I gotta go check in on my mama now."

Without waiting for No Name to utter banal pleasantries, PC pivoted and walked down the hall as fast as she dared.

As she was buckling her seat belt, her phone chimed. She glanced at the text. Rose. Rocky would have to spend at least the weekend in the city lockup. He couldn't be arraigned before Monday. No arraignment, no bail. Uncle Raymond was taking her home. That soured PC's mood. She thought she'd stop by to see her brother.

If Woody would let her.

Chapter 12

PC STOOD IN front of the holding cell. "You doing okay, Rocky?"

"They're promising three squares a day." He tried to smile. "Take out from any of the joints in walking distance. Had Chinese for lunch."

"I'm glad you're being well fed. Looks like you got the place to yourself."

The other three cells were empty.

"Yeah. Kinda quiet."

PC leaned in and whispered to her brother. "I've been told that your phone was found next to Heather Micah's body."

"I didn't kill her."

"I believe you, Rocky. That room where they found the body was empty. You were sleeping in there, weren't you?"

Rocky looked down. "Yeah."

"Your phone must have fallen out of your pocket while you were in the bed."

"Could have happened that way. I never have it turned on while I'm working. I don't suppose I'd know if it wasn't there."

"Exactly. Now, did Ms. Fennec say anything, or do anything that seemed odd to you?"

Rocky sucked his teeth for a minute. "Well, after you dropped me off, I came back into her office to ask you what time you were picking me up. You'd already left, but she did seem real upset. She was in her office, crying."

"Was she, now?" *Guilt for killing Heather?*

"I tried to cheer her up, but she just seemed…" He sighed. "Deflated, maybe. Like an old kickball that doesn't have enough air."

"Did you see her this morning?"

"No. She only works weekends if somebody calls in sick or something goes wrong. Least, that's what she told me, anyway."

What was she upset about Friday? Was she already planning her escape? "Thanks, Rocky. You've been a big help. I'll come back and check on you tomorrow."

"I'll be here."

At least Woody had the decency to stay in his office and not come bother us. She could see him sitting in there, pecking at a keyboard. PC almost stuck her head in the door but didn't think that would do anybody any good. *What would help was a nice walk. Take a little stroll around the square–there was plenty of time before she had to head back to Mama's to feed the critters.*

PC headed south from jail, past the Brisk Rib and the Lucky Wok. She stood at the intersection of Municipal Parkway and Main street. To her left, the giant craft brewery, the Biersal Brewpub, lay on Main Street. She was tempted to stop in and sample the wares, but shook it off. *Another time.*

She turned right on Main. A park, about an acre wide and two long, separated the city government offices from the county government ones. There were all the things one would expect to find in a rural hometown America city park–playground equipment, soccer field, a gazebo/bandstand, picnic area, and a fountain, with urns of trailing ivy and seasonal plants. Right now, red berry-covered hollies graced each concrete planter, and red velvet bows were getting bedraggled from the winter rain and winds. Probably well past time to bring in the holiday decorations.

She sat on a bench for a few minutes and watched some teenagers playing a pickup game of soccer, not really paying attention to them while she let a casserole of facts and ideas simmer into a theory on her mind's back burner. Then she got up and wandered back to the road. She noticed that across the street from the park was a hedge of roses. Even though it was January, they hadn't bothered going dormant, and a few pale pink and white blossoms peeked out of the leaves.

PC hadn't remembered there being a hedge when she was growing up, just a crumbling old Victorian house. It had been the fanciest house in three counties when it was built in the late 1800s, or so her grandmother had told her. The detective's eyes fell on a large white sign, held up by a pink brick plinth. The graceful curves of the wooden sign made PC think of a headboard for an antique bed.

Happily Ever Afters
Wedding Venue
Bed and Breakfast

Rose had said someone restored the old house. Good for them. She'd have to ask her mother for more details about it later. There were several done-up historical houses in Possumwood. She remembered going on field trips to the land grant empresario's mansion when she was in elementary school. And of course, the Historical Society had the Azalea Trail every spring that was a walking tour of houses from the nineteenth-century settlers.

PC kept walking. *Zeno's Pizza. Vintage Glory Antiques. Truffles!.* None of these places had been here back in the day. She felt like an old timer, where the world had moved on without her. How soon before she was shouting at kids to "Get off my lawn!"? She sighed.

Truffles! was on the north side of Main Street, and Drew's gallery was across from it on the south. PC was tempted to go in. Was it because she found the exhibit fascinating–or the proprietor? An icy gust of wind ruffled her hair, and a few fat drops of chilly rain splattered on the sidewalk. She slipped inside.

"PC!" Drew looked at his watch. "You're early. But I'm glad you could make it. Let me show you to our teaching room, and you can choose your materials. Naomi's only just arrived."

She gaped at him. *The workshop! I'd forgotten all about that. Now that I'm here, I can't just leave, but do I have time for this?* "Yeah. I, um… I—"

"Don't be nervous. It'll be fine." His warm hand on the small of her back was insistent.

PC stared at a small white glass owl on the counter as she weighed her options. She could insist on leaving. Or she could stay. Sometimes, when all the puzzle pieces flat out refuse to fit together, the best thing to do is something else. She was at a dead end, anyway. She had no authority to pull phone records to try to find where Fennec's phone was pinging. If No Name were unwilling (or unable) to tell her, there wasn't a lot she could do about it. Hiro might be able to help, but she had to wait for him to approach her. *Stay. Why not? It's only an hour.*

PC let Drew lead her back to the teaching room. There was no door. The space wasn't large, perhaps the size of a big living room. A paint-splattered double sink dominated the end closest to her, and a supply cabinet leaned against the opposite wall. Two plastic-covered eight-foot folding tables with three chairs each took up most of the free space in the room. The instructor was getting her materials ready and looked up when the two of them came in.

"Naomi, this is PC. She's one of your students today."

Naomi extended her hand. "Very nice to meet you."

PC couldn't think of anything that screamed "Artist!" more than Naomi. She had mermaid hair, a gradient of dark blue fading to sea foam green, a nose ring with a blue crystal in the center, and iridescent ear gauges.

Naomi helped PC set up her ink cake and brushes. The other five students, three women and two men, filed in and the instructor flitted away to help them with their supplies.

Once everyone was situated, she picked up one of her brushes. "Now. You hold the brush like this."

The class was almost over when PC heard the front door open and the clunk of something large dropping to the floor.

Then Drew's voice. "Mrs. Deen! Let me help you with that."

There were noises of people moving a heavy object around in the lobby.

Drew, again. "And how may I help you today?"

A woman's voice, Victoria Deen, surely, replied, "I'd like an appraisal for this."

"You only had to call–I would have come to your house. But you only just bought this piece…"

"I want to sell it–we've got too many paintings now–and I thought it would be easier this way."

"Of course."

Silence.

Victoria's voice. "I am so glad they made an arrest in Heather's murder. I feel so much safer now."

PC's ears pricked up, and she paused on her way to wash her brushes.

Victoria continued. "Well… I understand *you* haven't grown up here, but I, for one, am not at all surprised that Rocky Donovan killed her."

PC clenched her jaw.

"Really? Why is that?"

"Their father got killed when we were all in high school. Rocky never was right after that. You know, I saw him prowling around Azalea Manor on Thursday afternoon."

No, you didn't. Mama was the one who pointed out you weren't there. PC hastily rinsed her brushes so she could continue eavesdropping. The other students were already drifting out of the classroom.

Naomi beamed at her. "You did an excellent job, Ms. Donovan. Have you used watercolors before?"

"No. I mostly do acrylics. I really wish I could stay and talk some more, but I have to go feed my mother's animals. It was a fun workshop."

PC fumed as she left the teaching room. What right did Victoria Deen have to try to pin Heather's murder on Rocky and then act like he was some scary monster? *I've seen scary monsters, little girl, and you don't know the half of it.*

But getting angry wasn't going to solve anything, so she took a few deep breaths to compose herself.

She was calm as an icy lake by the time she got back to the lobby. Victoria Deen had left, but a large modern abstract oil painting leaned against the counter.

PC thought it was particularly ugly, but feigned interest, hoping to coax some information out of Drew. "Where did that come from? That's certainly a unique piece."

Drew chuckled. "A unique piece? That's typically what people say when they think a painting is ugly, but don't want to be rude."

"You got me there."

"A client brought it in for resale. Which is weird because they only bought it three months ago. Conceivably, one spouse liked it, and the other thought it was... unique."

PC smiled. "I enjoyed the workshop. Glad I came."

"If you're interested in grabbing a bite later..."

"I'm going to have to give you a raincheck. I really wish I could go. But with Rocky's situation, and all..."

"I understand. Next time."

"Next time."

PC half-jogged to her car. It was cold and drizzly now, and much darker than it should have been. Inside, she started the car and was glad she had sprung for the heated seats when she bought the SUV.

As she drove, her mind twisted and turned the new information she'd gleaned to try to make it fit with what she had already pieced together. Why would Victoria lie about seeing Rocky at the nursing home? He was an employee, so he was certainly there. But *she* wasn't. Or was she? What if she had gotten there early, encountered Heather, and confronted her about hitting on Reverend Deen? She could have killed her... and maybe Durelle Fennec saw it. Did she offer the director a wad of cash to skip town? Dead presidents can be very influential. That might explain why Victoria Deen had a sudden need for cash. Then again, perhaps she just hates the painting her husband bought, and Durelle Fennec is in a shallow grave somewhere. Or not. If so, Victoria was smart to never trust a blackmailer–they always get greedy, sooner or later.

PC pulled into Rose's driveway and groaned in exasperation. What she needed was to talk to Hiro Tran. She'd have to convince him to track down Director Fennec, because whether she was relaxing on a tropical island beach or decomposing in a forest, she held the key to getting Rocky released from the slammer.

Chapter 13

"How'd you sleep?" PC gave her brother a once-over. He was disheveled and puffy-eyed.

"Like a baby. If a baby was sleeping in a freezing room on a half-inch thick mattress that smells like vomit."

PC sighed. "I'm sorry. I'm doing the best I can to get you out of here. You've got your arraignment tomorrow morning-"

"They don't grant bail for murderers."

"Sometimes they do." *For a million dollars.* "Besides, your lawyer may argue it with the DA down to manslaughter, and you can bond out for that."

Rocky scowled. "I didn't do anything. I am not gonna plead guilty to a crime I didn't commit. I didn't even know Heather was in town, much less at Azalea Manor."

"Speaking of which... have you remembered anything at all about Durelle Fennec's behavior Thursday or Friday?"

"No. Like I said, she seemed upset on Friday morning, but she didn't tell me what it was about."

PC chewed her lip.

A whiney voice drifted in from the front of the cop shop. "I need to make a statement. About the murder." *Is that... Victoria Deen?*

"Yes, ma'am. Take a seat over there. Someone will be right with you."

PC raised a finger to her lips to shush Rocky, then tapped her ear. He nodded.

A male voice said, "Victoria? You said you needed to make a statement?" *Woody*.

"Yes! I saw him. At the nursing home on Thursday!"

"Okay. Calm down. Let's go into my office."

A door closed.

PC crossed her arms and exhaled hard. "What is she up to? You were working on Thursday, so it's no surprise if someone saw you there. The thing is, she wasn't there, at least not later, anyway, after the DB turned up."

"The what?"

"DB? Dead body. She seems to be going to a lot of trouble to pin this on you. You don't have any history with her, do you, that would make her try to hurt you?"

Rocky looked at the floor and rubbed his chin. "Not that I can think of… wait a minute. About ten years ago, I was here helping Mama with some stuff. I'd rode my bike down to the Silver Dollar for some liquid refreshment. I was on my way home, just turned onto Travis Street, when a Mercedes ran a stop sign and nearly hit me. They swerved at the last second and hit a fire hydrant. That was a big ole mess. Didn't do the car no good, neither. Anyway, the door opened and who steps out but Vicki Simon? I guess she was Deen by that point. Anyway, she was screamin' and hollerin' about how I got in her way and caused the accident. I did point out that she was the one who ran the stop sign, but she didn't wanna hear about that. I'd forgotten about it, though. But I guess I wasn't goin' to have to explain why I wrecked my new Mercedes in my ex-boy-friend's neighborhood."

"What? Who's her ex?"

"Well, you know the Parkers that live around the cor-ner from Mama?"

"We've met."

"Their nephew, Stuart, lived with them off and on while he was going to college. Vicki took up with him while she was waiting on Joshua to quit pining after Heather."

"Interesting. Seems a long time to hold a grudge, but..." PC shrugged.

As Rocky had predicted, the judge didn't grant bail at the arraignment. PC was keenly aware that if she didn't solve this case, her brother might be facing life in prison, or worse–headed for the Polunsky Unit in Huntsville. Death Row.

It was Tuesday afternoon before she could meet with Hiro Tran.

"You're not worried about someone noticing your car parked out in front of my Mama's house?" PC asked when he knocked on the door.

He laughed. "My girlfriend lives next door."

PC's brow furrowed. "Nothing wrong with dating older women, but isn't Mrs. Youn... married?"

"Of course. But her daughter, Annie, isn't."

"Ah. I'd never seen her."

"She's one of the dispatchers–she sometimes works weird hours."

"That would explain it." PC let out a breath. "I wanted to talk to you about Victoria Deen. I'm aware she showed up at the station on Sunday to give a statement about seeing Rocky at the nursing home. He'd just gotten a job there, so of course he'd be around. The thing is... Victoria wasn't there. Mama noticed she was missing while everybody was taking their seats, and I never saw her after the DB turned up. If she wasn't there, how did she see my brother?"

"Good question. Although your mom's not exactly an unbiased witness."

PC shrugged. "But she had no way of knowing that Heather was dead and Rocky was going to get blamed for it at the time." She reached for a three-ring binder. "I did find out who Bernadette was."

"Yeah?"

PC opened the binder and flipped through a few of the sheet protector-covered pages. "Her last name was Peyronel. She was in a lot of yearbook photos with Frank Smith, so they must have been close. Anyway, she left about halfway through senior year. Over the summer, she turned up dead on the side of the road just outside of Dallas, a victim of the I-35 Strangler. Although how this relates to Heather Micah, I have no idea."

"I had a conversation with Mr. Smith."

Irritated, PC closed the book. *What else is he holding out on me?* "And this didn't seem noteworthy?"

"No. He has an airtight alibi for the night of Heather's murder. And he told me all about Bernadette. Right before mid-terms that year, Heather asked him to give her his pre-cal homework to copy, and he refused. Out of spite, Heather told Bernadette that she was pregnant with Frank's baby. Distraught, Bernadette ran away from home, and ended up… well, you know what happened to her."

"Easy to see why Frank hated her."

"She didn't seem to be very popular around here, that's for sure."

"So why did she come back? She burned every bridge she ever crossed. Her mother died and her sister moved away. No one was welcoming her with open arms. So, why? I think if we can figure that one out, we'll have all but solved this case."

Tran gave her a sardonic smile. "You got a Ouija board?"

"If only it was that easy!" She frowned. "Just out of curiosity, has anybody filed a missing persons report on Durelle Fennec?"

"Not that I'm aware of."

Something else you're not telling me?

He suddenly glanced at his chest, then took his phone out of his shirt pocket. "That's Annie. She's home."

PC waved as if to shoo him away. "Go."

"Just so you know–Chief Wilson is going to request help from the Texas Rangers with the investigation. They'll probably be here by the end of the week."

"Thanks for the heads up."

She watched him walking toward the front door, trying to be careful and not knock over any of her mother's knickknacks that crouched on low shelves and odd end tables with his duty belt.

"Mama? Is there anything you need? I'm going out for a little bit."

"Could you bring back some cat food?"

"Sure."

The detective got in the car and drove out to Azalea Manor. She had a hunch. No one had reported Fennec missing, so her employer probably knew where she was, even if that waspish lady in her office refused to say.

When PC pulled into the parking lot, she noticed a woman sitting in her dusty car, putting on makeup. She got out and tapped on the window.

The driver's face came into view as the window retreated into the door. "Can we do this another time?" asked Director Fennec. She looked even more sad and tired than usual.

"Sorry to bother you, ma'am. Rocky's been arrested, and he's being held on suspicion of murder. You can corroborate his alibi—he needs all the help he can get right now."

Fennec sighed. "I just got back from my auntie's funeral. I need some peace."

"I understand that, ma'am. But if anybody could use a second, or third chance right now, it's Rocky. All the evidence against him is circumstantial, but it looks pretty bad."

Fennec closed her eyes and sighed again, a long, slow exhalation that rattled in her chest. "Fine. I'll go see him in the morning. Is he in county?"

"No, city jail."

"Okay. And I'll have a word with the chief while I'm there. Make a statement."

"Thank you so much."

"Sure, sure. Why don't you get outta here and let me get on with my day, mkay?"

"Of course." PC stepped backward. "But there's just one more thing. Do you remember seeing Victoria Deen here on the night of the murder?"

Fennec thought for a moment. "Now that you mention it, no. But I was busy doing other things."

PC took the long way around to Marberger's Grocery. Driving the back roads would help her focus on what pieces of evidence she had. She was glad that Durelle Fennec didn't seem to be involved.

Who had motive to kill Heather Micah? Might be easier to count people who didn't.

Means? Heather had probably been shoved, and she fell and hit her head on the metal bedrail. Doesn't rule out many.

Opportunity. Who was there at Azalea Manor on Thursday night? Rocky, of course. But he had no motive. Durelle Fennec? If she'd killed Heather, she probably wouldn't have come back to Possumwood from her aunt's funeral. Pastor Deen? If he had a motive, PC wasn't aware of it. It was entirely possible that someone else there for the sermon had an unknown motive, but Victoria Deen had been going to a lot of effort to pin the murder on Rocky. Was it that she just didn't like him, and her prejudice convinced her he was guilty? Was she covering up for someone else whom she knew or believed to be guilty? Or was she trying to deflect suspicion from herself? The only problem is that no one had seen her at the nursing home that night.

Now that the cavalry was coming, perhaps this case would get a move on. She had worked with several of the DPS investigators. They were top notch, but would they be able to dig up any more evidence than Possumwood PD already had?

The detective sighed as she pulled into a parking slot. It was still early enough that the store wouldn't be filled with shoppers stopping by to grab dinner ingredients on the way home from work, but not for much longer.

Her mother needed cat food, and Cordite was out of dental chews. She could make a targeted strike on the pet aisle and be done.

"PC! Are you still in town?"

She turned. Joshua Deen bore down on her from the housewares aisle with a box of lightbulbs in his hand.

"Yes. Helping Mama while she's getting over her hip surgery."

He tucked the box under one arm and took her hand in both of his, squeezing uncomfortably hard. PC flinched.

"I'm so sorry to hear about your brother." He released her hand.

"What have you heard?"

"That he killed that woman. That's why he's locked up, right?" His laser-whitened teeth gleamed behind a fake sympathetic smile.

PC bristled. "By 'that woman,' do you mean Heather Micah, your ex-girlfriend?"

"Heather was a troubled soul." His eyes narrowed. "We broke up a long time ago. I owe her a debt of gratitude, though. That breakup is what inspired me to go to seminary school. It changed my life." He looked at his right shoe.

"Did you see her while she was in town?"

He shifted his weight and changed his stance a little. "No. Not until the incident at Azalea Manor."

PC noticed a small dot of blood, about the size of an M&M, on Deen's oatmeal-heather thermal shirt, about level with his armpit and just above his left nipple. "What did you do to yourself? You're bleeding."

He looked down at his chest and swallowed. "Oh… we have the orneriest shrubs in town. I tried trimming off a wayward branch, but the bush won." Another fake smile. "I should probably go and get that in the laundry. It was nice to see you."

She watched him hurry out of the supermarket. He'd kept up his workout routine–still looked like a football player. She picked up the pet supplies and was on her way back to the car when her phone rang.

"What is it, Mama? Did you need something else from Marberger's?"

"No, honey. I need you to come home and help me. Guinevere's out again!"

Chapter 14

PC TOSSED THE grocery bag into the car. "Again? Alright, I'm just getting in the car. I'll stop by the Parker's on the way home."

"You do that. I'm gonna call Daisy and see if her boys can come help."

"See you soon."

Since Mr. Parker had told her he'd never hurt Gwen, well, not seriously, she felt less urgency than the first time. But still. It was not very neighborly to let your donkey chow down on someone else's prize roses.

She headed straight for the Parkers'.

To her dismay, the rose bushes had been heavily pruned, and there was not so much as a leaf or orange hip to attract a hungry burro.

Damn.

PC decided to take the cat food home and gather some donkey-wrangling supplies, namely molasses treats and a halter and lead, before she set out again. Also, a flashlight and a jacket would be handy.

Cordite was desperate to go outside, so she left the pet groceries on the table and snapped on his leash. As she followed his weaving around the yard, looking for the perfect place on the perfect tree, she wondered if he remembered anything from the nose work classes she'd taken him to. They hadn't practiced in... well, she couldn't remember the last time. But he had been an enthusiastic learner.

After he selected the prime spot and did his doo diligence, she took him inside and put the safety orange reflecting harness on him.

"Honey, what are you doin'? Now's not the time to walk your dog!"

"Mama, he's been to scent work class. Maybe he'll remember something and be able to track her. 'Cause I have no idea where to look. Mr. Parker's pruned his roses, so there's nothing for her there."

Rose smiled at Cordite, although she was a bit too unsteady to lean over and give him a pat. "You be a good boy and find my Guinevere. There's some chicken jerky in it for you if you do."

There would be chicken jerky, regardless. "Are you really trying to bribe my dog?" PC shook her head. "I'm going to get Gwen's halter and some cookies. Hopefully, we'll be back soon."

"Be careful. It's gettin' dark."

PC waved the Maglite as she dashed out the door, Cordite leading the way.

After she retrieved a feed bucket and tossed a handful of horse cookies into it, she had to hand over some treats to Arthur, the half-blind donkey, and Hazel, the tripod goat, since they made such a fuss the moment they heard the crinkle of the plastic bag. PC knelt down to give Cordite a good sniff of Gwen's halter.

"Find it!"

Cordite immediately began snuffling the ground, running in circles. He almost slid to a stop in front of one of the flowerbeds, then started digging in the azaleas.

"Cordite! Stop that!"

He snatched at something in the dirt before she pulled him away. It took PC a minute to figure out that it was an old, half-chewed pig's ear dog treat.

"I told her not to give you those. Drop it."

The dog lowered his head, disappointed. The decomposing ear tumbled to the ground.

"Don't worry. You'll get something better when we get back." She held the halter for him again and said, "Find it!"

Cordite put his sniffer to the grass and started following a zig-zag path. He bolted for the edge of the yard and PC jogged to keep up, not wanting to hinder his progress. The dog stopped under the big white oak tree and raised his head, sniffing. Then he raised his leg and peed on the tree.

"I guess you don't really remember much of scent work training after all."

The terrier put his nose down and tugged at the leash. She let him lead her down the street, not having much hope that he'd find Guinevere. But what else was she going to do? It wouldn't be any worse than her walking around with the flashlight and shaking the feed bucket.

Cordite didn't even slow down as he passed the Parkers' house. He paused at a crossroad and PC started to wonder if he was onto something. The dog chose a street and trotted off, PC jogging at the end of the lead heading towards downtown.

It was dark enough now that PC turned on the flashlight. She could see the lights of the Biersal Brewpub on the right a few blocks away, and a lighted gate on the other side of the street from it.

She shook the bucket. "Guinevere! Gwenny!"

There was no response. Cordite veered hard to the left.

Glad there's no traffic! Crazy dog.

She followed him. He was loping along on his short little legs, but he stopped suddenly from time to time to sniff at random things, nearly sending PC sprawling more than once. She could now read the sign in front of the lighted gate.

Happily Ever Afters.

Of course! They have that huge rosebush hedge.

"Gwenny! Guinevere! C'mon girl!" She shook the feed bucket. This time, she was answered by a snort and a loud *Eeeyaw!*

PC shone the flashlight along the hedge. About thirty yards away, she could see most of Guinevere protruding from the shrubbery.

"Get out of there, you nut!" She rattled the feed bucket again.

Gwen withdrew her head, chewing languidly. PC was dismayed at the size of the hole the donkey had made. Something was stuck in her thick forelock. At first PC thought it was a stick, but realized it was a bamboo knitting needle. Sparkles caught her eye, and she trained the flashlight along the bottom of the hedge. A trail of broken glass. Another ten feet or so down from where Guinevere had attempted to tunnel into the wedding venue, PC found a cellphone in the bushes. What was left of one, anyway. Someone had smashed it up pretty good.

She had no gloves or evidence bags, so she called Hiro Tran. Gwen enjoyed her cookies, as PC doled them out one at a time, while she waited for the officer.

Annie, the dispatcher, was in the car with him when he arrived ten minutes later.

"I'm sorry to interrupt your evening–I realize you're off duty– but I think I found Heather's phone."

The donkey brayed loudly. *Eeyaweeyaweeyaw!*

"Okay, technically, Guinevere found it."

"Isn't that your mother's burro?" Annie asked.

"Yes. She got out, looking for roses to devour, and found the phone, and Cordite found her. There's a knitting needle stuck in her forelock. You might want to take that in as well. And test it for blood."

"Blood? Okay, then. I hope it is Heather's phone. Still haven't gotten her records from the phone company."

"With any luck, the SIM will still be readable." PC scratched Gwen's shoulder. "Um, if you could keep my name out of this, I'd appreciate it."

"Why?" asked Annie.

"Woody–Chief Wilson–and I have... some history. It'll just make him mad, and I don't want him to take it out on Tran. Or take it up with me. Just better that way."

"The killer's number has got to be on that phone. You don't want any credit for closing the case?" Tran asked.

PC smiled. "No. I'm retired, remember? Anyway, I've got to get Guinevere home. C'mon Cordite. Let's go get that chicken jerky Mama promised you."

Besides, I'm pretty sure I know who the killer is.

Chapter 15

PC WAS CERTAIN she knew who, how, and when. She just didn't know why Heather was killed. She pulled out the manila folder that Tran had given her containing the photos of Heather's personal effects and spread the pictures out on her bed.

A carry-on roller bag.

Three outfits. All designer. All expensive.

Makeup, moisturizer, a toothbrush, and a tiny tube of toothpaste.

The eviction notice.

The storage rental receipt.

The newspaper clipping from forty years ago. Article about band funds being stolen. Continuation of the story about her father's murder and Coach Able's fatal car accident.

Heather had run out of money. She thought a quick trip to Possumwood would remedy that situation. The stolen band money couldn't have been more than a couple of thousand dollars, if that much. If she knew where that money was after all this time, or who had taken it, she wasn't likely to do more than break even, after the plane ticket and hotel. No, she was expecting a big payoff. And fast. Someone she knew would pay, perhaps because she'd blackmailed them before? Who had she made a point of visiting when she arrived?

She'd been kicked out of *Truffles!*, the Jorgensen's restaurant.

PC had witnessed her getting booted from Drew's art gallery.

Woody had picked Heather up from the gallery and taken her back to her hotel.

She'd gone to the Thursday evening service at the nursing home, so that could include any number of people. But no, there was one person Heather knew would be there, the one who ended up killing her. Someone with a deep, dark secret.

Hopefully, the killer's blood was absorbed by the porous bamboo knitting needle, and the crime lab could get enough of it out to test. The drop of blood found on the floor wasn't Heather's, and it didn't match anyone in CODIS. PC was fairly certain of who it belonged to, though there would need to be probable cause for a warrant to collect a cheek swab. DNA results didn't take the year or more to come back like they used to, but it still wasn't an overnight proposition. She needed to get the killer to confess, both so the DNA could be collected, and Rocky could be released. And the sooner, the better. All she needed was a plan.

It was Thursday evening and PC dropped her mother at the door of Azalea Manor, so she didn't have to navigate the shifting gravel. "Save me a chair, Mama."

"You know I will, honey."

PC parked and hesitated before she went in. She was either going inside to get a killer to confess or to make a complete fool of herself. And it would be streamed live on Reverend Deen's Justice Avenue Baptist Church's website for God and everybody to see. No pressure.

She took her seat next to Rose and looked around the room. So many people were there, hoping for a miracle. So was she. Just a different kind.

The piano music started up, and the audience clapped in time to it as Joshua Deen swept into the room. PC noted that Victoria stood sullenly near the cameraman.

"Is everybody ready," Joshua's voice boomed, "to make a joyful noise?"

The crowd clapped, and a few people whistled loudly.

"Let's bring down those healing vibrations!"

Those in the audience who could stand, did. Except for PC.

She scanned the room through two hymns and a short pep talk/sermon. Finally, Deen asked, "Is there anyone who would like to come forward for a hands-on healing?"

PC stood. The reverend's eyes narrowed as she walked up to the small, portable stage.

"How can the power of the Lord help you today, Primrose?"

"My brother has been arrested for a crime he did *not* commit. I want justice for Heather Micah, and I want to free Rocky."

"Sometimes people let us down and we don't want to believe the truth."

PC cleared her throat, ignoring Deen's words. "Heather came here to meet somebody. Your wife was worried about Heather texting you, wasn't she?"

"I would never be unfaithful to Victoria." The boom had gone out of his voice, replaced by venom.

"I never said you were. This is what I think happened. Heather came to Possumwood to collect a blackmail payment. But her intended victim had either had enough of her demands or never planned to pay. I don't think they intended to kill Heather, though." PC looked at Victoria, whose eyes widened. "There was a struggle, and she grabbed a knitting needle from a patient's yarn basket and stabbed her would-be mark. They shoved her, hard, and she fell and hit her head against the bed rail. Her neck snapped, and she was dead before she hit the ground. The killer then placed her body in one of the beds and covered her up before rejoining the Thursday service in the main lobby."

"If that's what happened, it sounds like an accident. But you don't know who this killer was, do you?" The smirk was more in his tone than on his lips.

"If it were truly an accident, most people would have called for help. People with nothing to hide, anyway. But this killer," PC looked pointedly at Victoria, "had no intention of letting Heather leave that room alive. Lot of folks in this town had good reason to hate her–she did some terrible things. But all of those were out in the open. Her killer had a secret so terrible that it could never be told. No one knew. Well, almost no one." She again looked at Victoria, who was now almost in tears.

Deen blotted his forehead and took a swig of water from the bottle on his podium. He manufactured a smile, "If it's so secret, how did *you* find out about it?" His chuckle rang hollow, and PC could feel every eye in the place on her.

"Heather was flat broke. She came here to raise some funds, and based on her luggage, she hadn't planned to stay long. Clearly, she believed her target would pay up quickly and without a fuss. Perhaps she'd extorted them before, and she understood how valuable her continued silence was."

Deen's eyes flicked to the cameraman, then back to PC.

"One of the items Heather had was an old newspaper clipping. The main story was about that time the band trip money was stolen. But that was just a coincidence. The story that mattered was the continuation of a front-page article. I believe she sent that part to her killer to persuade them to meet her. This article was about the night the Possumwood Panthers won the state championships."

Deen smiled, but it was pained, as if the light from his former glory hurt his eyes.

"I had to ask myself who could Heather have possibly been with that night. She was the head cheerleader, going steady with the football team captain, on the night of the biggest game in the history of Possumwood. She had to have been with you."

A broken sob escaped from Victoria, and PC watched her crumple into a chair. She wished it didn't have to be this way.

"Then I wondered what was it that she saw that the Reverend Deen would pay her lots of money to keep quiet. On the same night that the winningest coach ever swerved off the road and into a tree. I also wondered why your wife would lie to try to pin Heather's murder on my brother."

PC kept her eyes on the reverend, but he stared at his wife. Victoria was in a full-on ugly cry. PC felt bad for her. Her life was about to change dramatically, and not in a good way.

Deen looked down at his microphone, then gave a silent laugh as his mouth twisted into a bitter smile. "I guess I should have known it would catch up with me, sooner or later. With us." He glanced at his wife. "There was an after party when we got back to the school. Somebody managed to get champagne–don't know who, it was just there, and lots of it. I was wasted. All three of us were. Heather and I were going to drop Vicki off at her house before…" he shrugged. "My head was spinning, and I could hardly keep my eyes open. Then there was a bright light and a loud noise. I pulled over."

He took another gulp of water.

"I never sobered up so fast in my life as when I saw Coach Able's car wrapped around that tree. I did try to help. Couldn't get the door open, and the windshield was shattered. He was—" Deen closed his eyes and exhaled loudly. "It was obvious he was dead. I had my entire future ahead of me. What was going to happen if I got caught drunk, at the scene of a fatal accident, with two drunk, underage girls? I would lose everything. So we made a pact to never tell anyone. When Heather split, I married Vicki. What choice did I have, really?"

Not an ounce of regret for killing his coach or Heather. It was only ever about him. "You could have come clean at any time."

"Could I? And what would have happened to sweet Victoria? Should she have had our baby in jail? She was pregnant before we got married."

PC's head snapped to her left, to the sound of a scuffle. The cameraman was trying to wrestle a gun away from Victoria Deen. Hiro Tran and another officer appeared from Durelle Fennec's office, and the two of them disarmed her. As her hands were being cuffed behind her back, spittle flying out of her mouth, she screamed, "I hate you! I hate you! It was our secret! You ran Coach Able off the road! You killed him! And like a fool, I protected you all this time."

Hiro whispered in PC's ear as the second officer led Victoria away. "How'd you figure out it was her?"

"It wasn't."

Deen shook his head sadly. "Oh, Victoria. What have you done?"

"She hasn't done anything, other than help you cover up an intoxication manslaughter." PC snapped, suddenly tired of his faux concern.

"Are you making an accusation?" He batted his eyelashes, as if stunned.

"Confession is good for the soul."

"But I did confess. To some terrible decisions I made in my youth." He hung his head, mimicking shame, for a moment before he looked up with a sly smile. "Of course, the statute of limitations expired on that years ago."

"There is no statute of limitations on homicide. And even if there was, that wouldn't apply to Heather's murder. When the lab gets that knitting needle, they're going to find Heather's prints on the blunt end and your blood on the pointy end. How is that chest wound, by the way?"

Deen laughed out loud. "You can't prove it wasn't an accident. And the Mirabella DA couldn't figure out how to pour water out of a boot if the instructions were written on the heel." He held his hands out in front as Tran snapped on the cuffs.

Rocky rested on the couch, Cordite sprawled across his lap. The plate of crumbs from her brother's slice of 'Welcome Home!' cake on the coffee table. Several abandoned cups of ginger ale-sherbet punch surrounded it.

PC stood in the kitchen doorway, watching as Daisy, Rose, and Durelle Fennec chatted together, mostly about the brightened outlook for Rocky's future while he tried to pretend he wasn't listening. But she saw him steal a glance from time to time at the women, and a hint of a smile curl his lips.

Rose sat a little straighter. "You know what Lin Youn told me? She said that Travis Bailey took such an exception to the reverend's crack about how stupid he was that after he got done filing murder charges, he called up the IRS and pointed them in the direction of the church's accounts. Seems like there's something funny going on there."

Daisy perked up. "The Deens are cookin' the church's books?"

"They haven't had time to do their investigation, have they?" Rose gave Daisy a sharp look.

PC shook her head. *Always something.*

Cordite briefly raised his head when she turned and headed out to the back porch. Guinevere rested her jaw on the top of the wooden fence and looked expectantly at PC.

"Fine. But if you're going to keep up this level of cookie jackpot, you're going to have to keep solving cases." PC made her way to the feed room. Good thing there aren't many. Surely Possumwood was good for another twenty or thirty years without a homicide–that seemed to be the interval.

As she came out with a handful of cookies, she found that Arthur and Hazel had appeared next to Gwen. She passed out the treats and found herself scratching Guinevere's neck while the donkey chewed.

PC had deep roots in Possumwood. But it hadn't been home for a long time, even before she'd graduated high school and left town. Some hothead with a gun had ruined that for her. She thought of her house in Houston that suited her exactly. It would be some time before she was able to get back. While she was forced to be in Possumwood, she should make the most of her stay.

"Is it too late for a New Year's resolution, Gwenny?" She scratched the donkey's neck. "Maybe I'll make one after all. I resolve to find out who killed my father."

If you enjoyed this book, please consider leaving a review at your favorite book site. Reviews help other readers find and enjoy new books!

Other books by Holly Dey:

Manor of Death: The Possumwood Mysteries Book 1

Death on the Half Shell: The Possumwood Mysteries Book 2

Azalea Trail of Death: The Possumwood Mysteries Book 3

Death Re-Enacted: The Possumwood Mysteries Book 4

Death Rides a Bobcat: The Possumwood Mysteries Book 5

Key to Death: The Possumwood Mysteries Book 6

Death Curated: The Possumwood Mysteries Book 7

Pool of Death: The Possumwood Mysteries Book 8

All Death No Cattle: The Possumwood Mysteries Book 9

Death is Lager than Life: The Possumwood Mysteries Book 10

Art of Death: The Possumwood Mysteries Book 11

Little Town of Death-Lehem: The Possumwood Mysteries Book 12

Winter: Boxset Collection Books 1-3

Spring: Boxset Collection Books 4-6

Summer: Boxset Collection Books 7-9

Fall: Boxset Collection Books 10-12

Large Print Editions

Manor of Death: The Possumwood Mysteries Large Print Edition Book 1

Death on the Half Shell: The Possumwood Mysteries Large Print Edition Book 2

Azalea Trail of Death: The Possumwood Mysteries Large Print Edition Book 3

Death Re-Enacted: The Possumwood Mysteries Large Print Edition Book 4

Death Rides a Bobcat: The Possumwood Mysteries Large Print Edition Book 5

Key to Death: The Possumwood Mysteries Large Print Edition Book 6

Death Curated: The Possumwood Mysteries Large Print Edition Book 7

Pool of Death: The Possumwood Mysteries Large Print Edition Book 8

All Death No Cattle: The Possumwood Mysteries Large Print Edition Book 9

Death is Lager than Life: The Possumwood Mysteries Large Print Edition Book 10

Art of Death: The Possumwood Mysteries Large Print Edition Book 11

Little Town of Death-Lehem: The Possumwood Mysteries Large Print Edition Book 12